About the Author

William Prendiville is a journalist with a background in copywriting. He was awarded the Lionel Shapiro Award for Creative Writing at McGill University, Montreal, Canada. Born in Ireland, he now lives and works in Paris.

Atlantic Winds

WILLIAM PRENDIVILLE

Fairlight Books

First published by Fairlight Books 2019

Fairlight Books
Summertown Pavilion, 18-24 Middle Way, Oxford, OX2 7LG

A CIP catalogue record for this book is available from the
British Library

1 2 3 4 5 6 7 8 9 10

ISBN 978-1-912054-78-7

www.fairlightbooks.com

Printed and bound in Great Britain

Designed by Sara Wood
Illustrated by Sam Kalda
www.folioart.co.uk

To Aurie, Catherine, Jacqueline & Mary

Prologue

He had been walking for some time through the rain that washes in from the steel-grey Atlantic over the evergreens that run, as seen from above, like a livid and innumerable army from shore to shore. He must have come in at some point from the sky, across the water from the mainland, not directly to here, Bear Lake, but to the main airport some six hours north, then driven down.

People saw him come in, but few took notice. He drove down Main Street in his rented car, a neat grey Pontiac sedan, looking ahead, straight ahead, through the mountain mud that speckled his windshield. The small exploded bodies of mosquitoes, big-bellied, flying half drunk, sucked in by the whoosh of the car coming upon them like a tidal wave, were smeared upon the glass.

He stared through that mountain-dirtied windshield, driving up Main Street past the line of stores – Home Hardware, Fred's Furniture, the new unisex hair salon, the cinema (still closed) – without looking at them, without even seeing them or caring, as though he'd been living here for the past twenty years and was merely on his way home from work. His face was older, and exhausted from the trip. He looked a little ridiculous in the new clothes he wore, the collar of his navy-blue polo shirt turned up thoughtlessly, as though it really didn't matter to him what he wore, mechanically wore what everyone else wore and made no fuss or statement about it. He'd never been the type of person to make a fuss. He'd always been discreet, and this was perhaps one of the reasons everyone had liked him so much. He wore glasses now and that, with the neat new car, the upturned collar and the harried exhaustion on his face, gave him the air, in this blue-collar town, of a young professional. His neatly combed hair seemed to have expanded in the heat and humidity, before the clouds had been pushed by the cold air into the valley where Bear Lake lay and broke and it had begun to rain. But he was out of his car now and walking when a great peal of thunder exploded overhead and the rain came down in a greater deluge, and he strode back to his car through the guttering mud.

The rain fell heavily for some time while he waited, drumming on the roof, splattering on the windshield as the first few fat drops had on his glasses. It dislodged the mosquitoes, washing them away in streaming rivulets. It made, on his thin wide roof, an enormous sound. He sat, looking

8

through the rivulets at the gate before which he'd parked, its small wrought-iron insignia appearing in a droplet in the window, blurring away, then forming in another. His was the only car in the parking lot and it looked like something stranded, or like a person before a scene that everyone else had long abandoned.

Finally, when the thunderstorm had passed and the rain lessened, Tom swung open the heavy door of his car and got out. He was a tall man with a solid gait, although he looked awkward now stepping among the puddles with a jacket held over his head. The rain dripped along the branches and needles of the trees, making the air cleaner and cooler, so that the smell of spruce and pine was high in his nose and he could hear the isolated chirps of birds among the branches, darting from one tree to the next. His foot landed in a puddle but he didn't curse or even seem to notice; he left the muddied path and started moving through the uncut grass, his eyes now upon the older headstones, and occasionally the newer ones, shining beneath the white and black sky until he finally came to the plot where he knew it should be, the one headstone that he now stood before. He looked at it for a long time. The rain seemed to have cleaned the air itself, leaving no sound, brightening, as though with silence, the little cemetery that stood closed off from Main Street, and the new sections of town, and the old, warring neighbourhoods. He stared down at the white tombstone and its cheap gold lettering. It lay, a small thing, set further back among the older stones, ignored, wilfully forgotten. He knelt down to study it, with the face of someone who might have been earnest once but was no longer. With one arm, he held the jacket over him against the rain, and with the other, still kneeling, he reached out and began to trace the lines of the letters etched there – and perhaps for the first time since he'd arrived in town, or even since he'd arrived back from the mainland, he smiled, a little painfully. Perhaps not. Maybe he did nothing like that at all.

PART ONE

I

The day it all began Cormic and Tom were on Elizabeth Street, playing at Denis Brichard's. They hadn't gone there with any real purpose in mind and they certainly weren't there for Denis. The two sometimes went there randomly, when they were bored or hungry, simply because Denis was about the same age and lived down the street from the slightly younger boy, Cormic. 'Let's go to the Brichards',' Tom had said off-handedly, and so there they'd gone. There wasn't a great deal else to do in town.

Often they would go to the woods behind Cormic's house, or bike along Elizabeth Street. Or they would hang out across town by Tom's, up by their school and the house with the high hewn-stone fence; when younger still, they used to climb over it at nights to steal crab apples, that is until the owners had finally had enough of that and directed a spotlight from their back door over the tree, after which Tom had declared it was not worth bothering with it anymore. For he had been, even at ten, of a judicious slant of mind, able to weigh options and judge the costs – Tom, the brightest boy in class and singled out in Grade Five for advanced tutoring in sciences and maths. He never bragged about it or saw anything special in it, even if his mother, who was a teacher at the same school, did. So everyone would say how good Tom was, how intelligent, how talented – oh, what an admirable child. 'I hear you're doing very well in school, Tom. Now if you could only teach my son how you do it,' Cormic's mother would joke when he was visiting, at which Tom would smile patiently and look slightly annoyed.

The two boys had met when Cormic first arrived from the mainland. During the morning recess of Cormic's first day, he'd been pushed into a race among a group of boys and had come in a close second, with Tom beating him by an extended stride. Tom had turned to the new boy afterwards with a kind of joyful admiration, and later, as Cormic was walking home, had overtaken him, walking fast from behind with his school bag slung casually on his shoulder, and exclaimed, 'That was a good race. Where are you going? You going down the hill? I'm going here,' he said, pointing right at the top of the hill, where a street led down towards his home. 'My name is Tom. Clairbourne. Good race! See you tomorrow.'

That was in Grade Five, Cormic's first year here, and they'd been friends ever since. Cormic was too young then to see the darkness in him, beneath a certain flippancy, or his manner in games they later played with girls, in which lots would be drawn and couples matched behind a shed near the school grounds, to kiss awkwardly. Of all the boys, Tom alone would go further, emerging afterwards with the girl from behind the shed with a look on both their faces like the shadow of a shared secret. Even in Grade Five Tom was not only the most intelligent in the class but the most attractive to the girls, though he didn't seem to care for any. It wasn't callousness per se but more a kind of general and indiscriminate disregard that seemed at times as broad and munificent as the sun.

And so, 'Let's go to the Brichards',' Tom had said that afternoon – the boys were fourteen now – because they'd already whiled away the better part of the day on their ten-speeds at the corner shop doing nothing, and Tom had not wanted to go home yet. Nor had Cormic, so the two thought they would spend the rest of the afternoon in the basement room at Denis Brichard's watching TV, until it was dinner-time.

It was a hot and bright summer day. They pulled in to the house and laid their bikes on the front lawn and walked up the steps. The house was the only one on the street so deeply varnished, a bit like Denis, whose mother would constantly dress him in various shades of brown. Mrs Brichard was delighted they'd shown up. 'Come in, come in,' she said, stepping back from the front door and ushering them inside, as if scared they might change their minds. 'Denis!

Denis!' she called excitedly downstairs. 'Your friends are here!' which must have confused Denis somewhat, for the two rarely came and he otherwise spent the majority of his time alone, among his own games and inventions, in his basement den. They found him there now, absorbed in one of his sci-fi books.

'Hey guys...?' he said, lifting his head, a little confused, for apparently he had either ignored or not heard his mother, his eyes having a kind wondering look behind cheap glasses, as though he was peeping out, startled, from another world.

The two boys dropped on either side of him on the old L-shaped couch in front of the TV.

'Hey Denis. Whatcha doing?'

Cormic picked up the remote and turned on the TV.

'What're you reading?' Tom asked.

'Frank Herbert.'

'Let's see,' Tom said. 'Oh, I've read that! It's good, eh? Do you have any cookies?'

Denis looked embarrassed. 'My mom won't let me have 'em. She says I eat too many.'

'Do you think *we* could get some?' Tom asked.

'She also says I drink too much pop,' he said, ignoring him.

'Do you think we could get some, Denis?' Cormic repeated.

'Okay. If I say it's for you. Do you think I drink too much pop?'

'I don't know, Denis,' Tom said. 'How much pop do you drink?'

'A lot,' Denis said, crestfallen. He went upstairs and came back down with a platter of milk and cookies his mother had proudly prepared.

They watched TV for a while and ate, then Denis wanted to show them a bike he was trying to make and they went upstairs and through a side door into the garage, which was in the same dis-array as the basement. Denis had taken an engine from an old lawnmower, which lay in a discarded heap in the corner, and attached it to an old BMX bike, the type that Tom and Cormic had stopped riding years before.

'See,' Denis said, bent over where the bike lay like some wounded animal on the garage floor. He was really talking to himself now, tinkering with the engine: 'I can't get that' – a wire – 'matching with this...' A grease stain had appeared on his cheek; he wiped his face with the back of his hand. 'Don't you think that if I put that there it will move? I don't know why it doesn't move. Ah, there, it moved! Did you see it? It's good, it moved.' Tom had wandered away while Denis was explaining this and stood looking out of the front of the garage. He seemed to suddenly startle as he leaned forward into the sun-light, like something perched.

'Hey, Denis, Denis, Denis...' he called. 'Who's that?'

Cormic followed Denis to the front of the garage and saw the girl from across the street – saw her, really, that is, for the first time. She was walking with her shoulders sloped, carrying brown bags of groceries from a truck towards the house. Her father slammed the door of the truck behind her and followed with more bags. He stopped for a moment, looking back, and called out in a deep, thundering voice, 'Tina... *Tina!*' A huge, brown, ugly mongrel bounded out from the other side of the truck and followed them up the stairs.

'That's the Dovonovitches.'

Tom stood unmoving in the sunlight from the garage door, watching until the front door crashed behind them. He even remained for a moment after they had disappeared, with a vague air of consternation, then, pushing down whatever had been set loose inside him, he turned back to the garage where Cormic and Denis were bent over the engine again. He stared down at the bike and, with that troubled look on his face now gone, or rather, compassed from a broad general confusion to the more circumscribed problem at hand, he bent down, tightened two bolts and pulled the cord. Then he stood back, contented, while the sound of the engine filled the garage, like a buzzsaw.

II

Bear Lake, the town, lay in a valley on the lake that gave it its name. The nearest city was an hour's drive away. That distance was halved by a tiny hamlet on the highway, where there was a roadside convenience store Cormic and his family would stop in for gas on the way to or from skiing. Cormic's father used to make house calls between these two populations, moving along the highway that cut through the forest like a faded scar. Sometimes Cormic would go with him on his house calls out to Trout Bend, the halfway hamlet, while his younger sisters and mother remained home. The jeep would dip along the island's highway, turning in to dirt roads, the headlights seeking out houses through the dark, barely creeping at times when the snow had fallen so thickly it raised everyone feet from the earth and lay stacked upon the long arms of the trees that stood as hardy, silent and unbending as the people scattered among them.

Cormic and his family had come over from the mainland when he was ten and moved into the house down the street from the Dovonovitches'. Theirs was a three-storey tumbledown with cheap blue and white siding on the top levels, and a front lawn of unkempt grass with an old oak rising in the south corner. The first unpainted level was little more than a shed used to house the lumber they kept against the island winters, when mountainous drifts of snow and ice seemed to fasten every home into stoic isolation. Unpainted pine steps reached up the front of the house to the second level, where there was a living room and kitchen and, beside them, the sister's room, closed off from the world. Two large windows stared out on to the street from the third floor, where Mr and Mrs Dovonovitch's, and their daughter Sasha's, bedrooms were squeezed in beneath a low roof, so that, despite the apparent size of the house from the street, the living quarters were in fact much smaller than they looked. It had been a foreboding place, because it seemed to almost proudly magnify its own disrepair, and not least because of the elliptical warnings that their neighbour and the town gossip, Mrs Ball, used to give out about the old family that lived within.

'Sure,' she would say, sharing tea with Cormic's mother in the kitchen, 'Frank Dovonovitch is a lovely man when he's in a good mood, and it's no matter that he's not always in a good mood, for when he is, he's sure enough to say to me, should I pass him downtown, "Good day, Tina" – not Mrs Ball, mind you, my God-given name by marriage, but Tina, like his dog, not the nicest thing, but I don't mind, you see, so long as he's polite when the occasion calls... May I?' – reaching for the sugar – 'Thank you. I only take a spoonful. You're very kind... But there are others now, I won't mention their names, that'd be *untoward*, who aren't as kind as myself, who'll tell you all kinds of awful things about him... But you mustn't listen, you mustn't listen to gossip around here, my dear, it's a dreadful habit. As for me, I try to keep my nose out of it. These others, they say – and let's leave them unnamed for now, you'll gets to know them soon enough – they say that they keep that daughter of his – not the younger one, the younger one's a dote, lovely child! – in some closet because they're too afraid to show her the light of day. "It's God's curse upon them because he's an evil man," they say. "He is. He fiddled with her when he grew tired of his own wife, and look at the result." God love the younger one when she comes of age! Now, that's what *they* say. I'm content to bid him "Good day" when he says a good day to me. I do feel pity for the child, though, if half of what is said is to be believed. Ah, dear, it's a terrible, *terrible* world we live in sometimes... Would you have another drop?'

'I wouldn't listen to a word of what that woman says,' Cormic heard his father say after Mrs Ball had left. 'Mr Dovonovitch is a patient of mine, and while he may be gruff, he's hardly capable of doing the things he's being accused of. It's not the first time I've heard it. You need to be wary, Marie, of the gossip that circles in a little town like this. Soon, it'll start circling around us.'

She agreed, but later, when he was gone, she took Cormic aside. 'You must never go to that house alone. Okay, Cormic? Never,' she said, putting a hand on his shoulder. 'Not even with your friends.'

*

Cormic had occasionally seen the 'younger one', 'the dote' – that 'lovely child', Sasha – before on his way home from school, but they had never spoken. She was something of a tomboy, with dark-brown hair cut above the nape of the neck, a little grubby, most always playing alone, and apparently content to do so. Sometimes he saw her walking with her friend from the end of the street on the way to or from school (he and Tom went to St Clair's at the other end of town, she and her friend went to the public school nearer Elizabeth Street) and sometimes he might see her on the front lawn of her home playing with the huge mongrel, which would bark at anyone who passed too close, but for the most part he didn't pay her much mind – there were other things to consider: bikes, TV, games. She was also a year younger than him and his friends, unworthy of attention, until the summer Tom saw her from Denis's garage.

One moment he would always remember, from those first years, when she was to him just a stranger who lived in the house his mother had told him to avoid. His father had to make an urgent call to her family's house one evening while his mother and sisters hadn't come back from shopping in Corner Brook, the city about an hour's drive away. Cormic was in his room and his father was in the living room, his legs raised on the sofa-chair, after a long day of work, when the phone rang.

'Hello?' he heard his father say from the phone in the kitchen. 'Yes. Yes... Is she breathing?... No. No, don't give her any food... Yes. Okay. Right away. Five minutes. Goodbye.'

He heard his father pass down the hallway to get his things, then looked up and saw his father staring at him for a moment in the bedroom doorway. 'Come on,' he said. 'Put on your jacket. I've got to make a house call.'

His father carried his small, black doctor's bag, and they walked out the front door and down the street in the dusk and turned right in to the Dovonovitches'. Mrs Dovonovitch, a fat blond woman with a red face and pale blue eyes, answered the door. 'In here,' she told his father, pointing to a door beside the kitchen, through which Cormic's father now passed and from behind which came a shrieking of such violence that it set Cormic's hair on end.

The interior of the house was ill-lit and dirty. Cormic stood in the hallway, at the bottom of the stairs, across from the door, from which Mrs Dovonovitch now ran out. She carried a basin of liquid that slopped to the floor, with scraps of food that had been vomited or thrown, poured it into the kitchen sink and returned again, opening and closing the door behind her. No one was paying Cormic much mind, between the running about and the thumping and horrendous violent, endless, shrieking. Not long after, Sasha appeared in the stairwell above him, having come from her room, where she'd been sent during the commotion. She must have been eleven then, a year younger than him at the time, and she stood at the top of the stairs, looking down: a little dark-haired girl with bright and shy blue eyes, skin so dark it looked grimy, a pair of old cords and a grubby yellow-flowered t-shirt. She seemed startled to see him there and to not want to show it. She didn't look worried about the commotion, however, as though it was something she was used to. 'Hi,' she said awkwardly. 'Hi,' he said, just as awkwardly, then she went into the kitchen and came back out with a glass of water, smiled at him with the same look of shy embarrassment and passed back up the stairs.

There came a loud thump from the room and a melee of raised voices, followed by a sudden calm, like a doldrum. The door eventually opened and Cormic's father emerged with Mr Dovonovitch, a man twice his size, with a heavy face and deep wrinkles burrowed into the back of his neck, where his hand kept returning, as though by habit, as though he were still outside, swiping away the black flies. He looked at Cormic and said nothing. The bedroom door was left open behind them and Cormic saw the cause of that earlier shrieking. Propped up on a bed in the corner sat a large woman with pale skin slicked with sweat, hair so orange it was luminescent and the same pale blue eyes of her mother, calm and wondered now, guileless and content. Mrs Dovonovitch was sitting on a chair beside the bed, trying to feed her again.

'You'll have to watch her for a while,' his father was saying. 'Be sure to give her the medicine I gave you, twice daily.'

'Yes,' Mr Dovonovitch said.

'If it happens again, call me directly. I only live up the street.'

'I know.'

'Have you met my son?' his father asked.

'I've seen him.'

'Hello,' Cormic said.

'Nice to meet you, boy,' he said without smiling, and wrapped a huge hand over Cormic's.

Mrs Dovonovitch was still trying to feed her daughter in the room behind, and Cormic could hear her saying, as they turned to leave, 'There, there, my love, now, you're doing better, one more... one more... there... there...' spoon-feeding her 200-pound daughter who remained, according to the town, confined for ever to that room, and who was gurgling now, placated, with the eyes of a suckled child.

It was night when they left, and as he followed his father back up Elizabeth Street Cormic turned and saw a single light on upstairs, where Sasha had gone, bright against the dark.

III

Tom was always at Denis's now. He didn't want to go there to watch TV but instead found excuses for Denis to stay out in the garage or on the front lawn, waiting to catch sight of Sasha while pretending not to. In the moments she happened to appear, he would, if they were sitting on the front steps, stand to stretch himself so she might see him; and on one occasion, when she appeared while the three boys were throwing the Nerf football on the front lawn (a game Tom had organised), he near broke his arm by making a diving catch, though Sasha didn't seem to notice him.

'One more throw, Denis,' he called out urgently afterwards.

'I'm tired...' Denis said.

'One more...'

'I don't want to play anymore.'

'Cormic,' he said, turning and keeping half an eye on Sasha going up the front stairs of her house, her head down, 'Cormic, throw me the ball! Throw me the ball!' until she disappeared.

There was, however, one moment she finally did seem to see him, when, stepping out of her father's car one day, she suddenly turned and looked at him quizzically, as though, with a kind of female fearlessness, she was demanding to know what he was doing. All pretence in Tom dropped away and he stood staring at her with his face drained of everything but fear. They stood there for a moment, staring at each other as though across a great divide, until a car door slammed, her father appeared and Sasha turned away again, walking on ahead of her father up the front stairs without once looking back.

'I've got to meet her,' Tom said.

She emerged again about a half-hour later, and although the sun was falling and there was a growing nip in the summer air, she'd changed into a white summer dress with a red sweater looped about her shoulders. The dress made her dark skin look darker, and as Tom stood stock-still and watched her descend the front steps, she glanced at him ever so timidly, ever so fearfully, then turned up the road with her long arms swinging awkwardly beside her, like she didn't know what to do with them, and hurried away, as though with fear at what she'd just allowed herself to do. They watched as she turned in to Cindy Bennet's house at the end of the street.

*

Summer passed, and Tom never mentioned Sasha again after that day he'd said to Cormic, not with desperation but with a kind of declared certainty, 'I've got to meet her,' so that you might well have thought he'd forgotten about her, as he forgot about the girls he kissed behind the shed by the school.

He graduated into high school, which meant he saw Cormic less than he had over the summer or the years before, because they had different classes now. But Cormic was in Tom's mother's math class, and he told Tom how she would brag about him; the whole school knew she bragged about him, knew already who he was, it seemed, though he was only in Grade Nine. It caused Tom enormous embarrassment. Cormic said that she would stand at the board before some difficult equation, her face disfigured by the polio that had struck her decades before and had left her with a distended left eye and a frozen squint, and say to the whole class, without any particular reason, 'You know, my son Tom does these all the time, very easily. He has a real gift.' *'He has a real gift!'* others would mimic to him later in the hallways, at which he would stand still and look at them and say nothing. But it made him angry, even if he didn't show it then, and he told her so.

'Son, I'm just very proud of you,' she said, and he stared at her and hung his head.

Tom mostly saw Cormic now during volleyball team practices, where, though he wasn't good enough to make captain, he was on constant rotation, and the two would walk home together after practice in the same way they'd walked home together after classes in elementary school, the high school being simply a larger building on the same fenced grounds.

They were walking home after practice one day in early September and had stopped at the place where their ways parted at the top of the hill, where Cormic would turn off left and Tom turned right, where the road continued down and joined the main street that led out of town. Autumn was beginning, and from where they stood you could see the town stretching out under its softer light, the lake shimmering to the east and the highway moving off beside that, into endless trees.

'Do you know the Bennetts, who live at the end of your street?' Tom suddenly asked Cormic. 'Their daughter's friends with Sasha.' He said the name casually, off-handedly, as though it was already something he was long used to saying.

'No,' Cormic said, looking at him, surprised, and shook his head.

Then, later that same week, as the two were walking home again after practice, Tom asked, 'Do you want to go see that new movie, *Star Wars*, on Saturday?'

'Sure,' Cormic said.

'What do you think about the matinee?'

'Good.'

'Oh,' Tom said then, 'Cindy Bennett and Sasha Dovonovitch are coming, too.'

Tom spoke to her for the first time in front of the cinema on Main Street – the only cinema in town, with a huge marquee that was, even then, never lit. The 'date', as it were, was not at all what anyone expected, except Tom, who had orchestrated it with a sort of cunning and patient wilfulness. He had arrived early with Cormic and stood beneath the marquee, quietly waiting for the girls to arrive. He was anxious, though he tried not to show it, kicking up stones in front of the cinema with his hands in his pockets, looking up Main Street and occasionally turning and looking behind him in case they'd decided to take the long way round. When he finally saw them walking up the sidewalk, he pulled his hands from his pockets, straightened up and fixed a smile on his face that, he knew, beamed with a sort of false arrogance.

Cindy smiled at him, for Tom was, as far as she knew, her 'date'. He had accosted her downtown and it was she who'd proposed the double date. 'Sorry we're late,' Cindy said, unapologetic. Then she smiled and said sarcastically, in a way much beyond her years, 'My mom always told me it's good to keep a man waiting...' Her hair was curled, and she wore pink lipstick and large looped earrings. 'This is Sasha,' she said, gesturing to her friend.

'Oh, that's okay,' Tom said, glancing nervously at Sasha. 'We have time,' and then immediately lost his earlier arrogance, the smile remaining on his face like a broken toy. 'Do you know Cormic?' He turned to Sasha abruptly, almost aggressively, after they had stood for a while in awkward silence.

'Yes,' Sasha said, timidly. 'You came to my house once with your dad.'

'A long time ago,' Cormic said.

She was wearing the same white summer dress she'd worn before, though it was cold out now, with a motley-coloured autumn jacket that looked new and sat on her boxily.

'I'm Tom,' Tom said, suddenly regaining his confidence.

'I know,' Sasha replied, 'Cindy told me,' and looked away, blushing.

Cindy looked at Tom and Sasha and suspicion flashed in her eyes. 'Do I have time for a smoke?' she asked suddenly.

'Sure,' Tom said without much interest, then remembered himself and teased. 'You shouldn't smoke, Cindy,' he said, smiling for her.

Cindy smiled at the attention, then turned away coquettishly, brandishing her cigarette. 'Tom told me you're on my street,' she said to Cormic.

'Yes.'

'Weird I've never seen you before,' she declared, and smoked. 'I've lived on Elizabeth Street my whole life – with Sasha.'

'I moved there about four years ago…'

'Hmm,' she said, eyeing Tom and Sasha again, who were standing beside them in awkward silence. In line, Tom kept up appearances and stood beside Cindy, but he kept turning around to keep Sasha in the conversation while she stood meek, glancing at Cindy uncomfortably.

'So, you two are in the same class?' Tom asked.

'Sash is a year below me,' Cindy interjected.

'Did you guys grow up together?' he asked Sasha.

'We've known each other our whole lives,' Cindy answered.

Tom looked at her with irritation and smiled wanly. Sasha had said very little. Once inside, he sat beside Cindy, impatient for the film to end, his thoughts hardly distracted by the intergalactic battle between Good and Evil taking place on the screen before them, glancing across Cindy now and then to where Sasha sat stiffly staring ahead, conscious of being watched. At one point, Cindy shifted closer to him, resting her thigh against his. He stiffened and glanced at her with a frozen smile that looked something like fear and left his leg there for the rest of the film with confusion and a sad air of defeat.

Being outside again after the film had ended came as something of a relief, following the tension in the cinema. But Tom wasn't going to let everything end so easily. 'How about a soda?' he asked Cindy as they stood awkwardly before the cinema, as though, indeed, the question was for Cindy alone. There was no time to lose now and as soon as Cindy warily agreed, he negotiated things so that he was walking ahead with Sasha while Cormic was left behind to walk with Cindy, who grew increasingly outraged, although she tried to pretend she didn't care.

'Nice shirt,' she told Cormic as they walked behind, trying to make conversation.

'Thanks.'

'You probably got it at Daly's,' she told him with an affected air, Daly's being the one expensive clothes shop on Main Street.

'I think my mom got it in Corner Brook.'

'Where in Corner Brook? *I* go there all the time,' she said, and added loudly, so Tom could hear, 'I had a boyfriend up there!'

'I don't know,' Cormic told her.

'Probably the new mall,' she assured him. 'Sash…' she called ahead. 'We should go to the mall.' Pointedly ignoring Tom now. 'I'll bring you. I'll get my sis to drive *me and you*.'

'Okay,' Sasha said, and looked at Tom, embarrassed. Tom, meanwhile, was peppering her with questions, as though letting her lapse into silence would be worse than a setback, a defeat. He spoke with a hurried, authoritative air.

'So, you go to school with Cindy?'

'Yeah.'

'Do you like it?'

'It's okay…'

'Did you like the movie? I thought it was pretty good,' he said, without letting her answer. 'Whoosh, whoosh.' He gesticulated jokingly, waving an imaginary lightsaber. 'Did you like it?'

'M-hmm.' She nodded, watching him.

It was clear to everyone now what was happening,

but Tom didn't care – he was talking to Sasha, and that was what was most important. They walked two steps ahead, speaking to each other as though they were alone, while Cindy and Cormic lagged behind in silence. They had walked from the cinema to the nearby hotel, the nicest building in town, with a cheap neo-Georgian façade, where executives from the paper and pulp company stayed when they came to visit operations in Bear Lake. The dining room was empty when they entered and they sat at a table by the front windows, looking much too young to be there. Sasha and Tom already seemed, in the silence that had settled between them, somehow set apart. A slight flush had risen on Sasha's cheeks, and her eyes, whenever she dared glance at Tom, sparkled with a sort of nervous happiness. And Tom felt more himself again, calmer, more at ease than he'd ever felt before. He was looking through the menu now. 'How about a Coke float?' he asked her. 'You should try one. They're really good here.'

'Okay,' Sasha said, and Tom felt, in that assent, a small, first triumph, a sudden intimacy briefly shared between them.

They ordered. The drinks came and Tom instructed the waitress. 'That's a soda there and a soda there, and two floats here,' he told her, smiling at Sasha. He was too confident now. 'We should start a club,' he told Sasha, at which she smiled uncomfortably beneath Cindy's surly silence.

Cindy rolled her eyes and groaned.

'Do you smoke?' she demanded of Cormic.

'Uh, no...' he apologised.

'Do you smoke?' Tom now asked Sasha, seeking desperately for something to say, to start a conversation of any sort.

'No,' she said.

'You should start a club,' Cindy quipped.

'Sure,' Tom quipped back, 'but this time I'll let girls in,' at which a frank and simple laugh erupted from Sasha, as though in spite of herself. She seemed even embarrassed by it, blushing slightly, and Tom suddenly looked at her with a proud, loving and surprised air.

But all that suddenly changed, that gentle bridging of the gap between them seemed to spin off for good, when Sasha next looked up; the blush on her face disappeared in a spasm of fear, and voices exploded behind them. The words were muted against the hotel window but they could see, standing in the parking lot outside, Mr Dovonovitch's huge, still back in the sunlight like a monolith. A thin grey-haired man with metal-rimmed glasses and a pale face, with two other men on either side, was staring up at him indignantly while another, standing beside Mr Dovonovitch, his back also turned to the hotel window, was shouting at them violently. The three men facing the window were wearing suits and carrying briefcases, and the thin man with the glasses staring at Mr Dovonovitch had a look on his face (he was British, as they found out later) of apportioned tolerance that was reaching its limits. As for Mr Dovonovitch, he didn't even appear to be speaking. He stood unmoving as his friend shouted; only once did he raise his arm, point a finger at the men before him and then lower it again like a lever, after which one of the other two businessmen exploded with rage. Then Mr Dovonovitch turned his back to them and walked away. He looked like he had just come from work, although it was a Saturday. His dark hair stood up like spikes at the back of his neck and he wore, over his collared shirt, a faded lumber jacket with sawdust still clinging to it. He seemed, as he passed the window, by his height, by his weight, by the dark skin that was almost burnt black and his dark blue eyes, which were the same, indeed, as Sasha's, like a giant from some foreign country. He passed without looking in, expressionless, leaving the others shouting behind him. He got into his truck, the sound of the shutting door thumped against the hotel window – Sasha jumped a little – then he drove away.

'Cindy,' Sasha said, 'I-I've got to go.'

'Okay, Sash,' Cindy told her, with immediate resolution.

She seemed to have forgotten Tom was even there now. She stood and said hurriedly, 'Goodbye.'

'Thanks for the movie...' Cindy said to Tom ironically as they left.

And before he could even fully stand, Sasha was gone, leaving behind her, after she'd hurried to pay, a small plastic tartan purse gleaming on the table, like something planted there by Fate itself, while Tom sat stunned, staring after her silently, his face set, as against a wind.

IV

'Sure, it'll be the end of us!' Mrs Ball declaimed to Mrs Marshall, Cormic's mother, over tea. 'Can you imagine Bear Lake without it? It's the butter to our bread. Ah no, no, no,' she said, shaking her head. 'Mark my words, if what they say is true – and I'm not saying it is, mind you, because I'm not one to listen to gossip – sure, you might as well pack your things now and head back to where you came from. We'll be little more than a ghost town here, full of drinking men and weeping women. Didn't it happen in Stephenesville? That was a boomtown before the logging shut down. Look at it now – it's not fit for a mouse. Take away a man's job and you take away his soul, and we poor women are left to pick up the pieces. Ah no, no, no, if there's any truth to those rumours, we're done for. Done for!'

'I haven't heard about anything more than a number of lay-offs among the temporary lumberers,' Cormic's father said.

Mrs Ball smiled, indulgently. 'Now would you

go and tell yer new doctor you were about to lose your job when ye barely knew him?'

'I've been here for four years, Tina,' he told her.

'Four years is a glint in a baby's eye,' she said shortly, then proceeded to direct her attention to his wife again.

This, in any case, was how they'd heard about it, through Cormic, a couple of weeks before Guy Fawkes Night, when news of the cutbacks among the loggers, and rumours about the closing of the International Pulp, Power and Timber company, the IPP&T, spread through town like wildfire.

Several weeks had passed since the 'date' at the movies, and Cormic had seen Tom only a few times since that moment when Sasha had abruptly stood and left, leaving behind the purse that Tom had afterwards held with a look of stunned concern as he'd watched her disappear, turned it over and over in his hand until he'd finally put it in his pocket.

Every time he'd come over to visit Cormic since then, Tom appeared both distracted and agitated, and left as restless as he'd arrived. There never seemed to be any purpose to his visits. He appeared unannounced at the front door as though he'd come as an afterthought, on a decision made in an empty moment, which was indeed the case, for he had cycled up Elizabeth Street, with the purse in his pocket, not to visit Cormic but to visit Sasha. He only continued on to Cormic's when he'd lost the courage to go to hers. But he didn't say anything about that to Cormic.

He only arrived at the front door unexpectedly, with a frown he couldn't hide. 'Hey,' he'd say with forced breeziness, the purse still hidden in his pocket. 'What are you up to?'

'Hello, Thomas,' Cormic's mother would call.

'Hello, Mrs Marshall. Hello, Mrs Ball,' politely, dutifully.

'Well, now, that's Mia's boy,' Mrs Ball would say as he passed. 'If he's anywhere near as bright as she claims he is, he'll be the premier of this island soon enough, if Mia has anything to do with it! Ha ha ha... God love the child!'

But Tom never appeared to hear any of it. His mind was always elsewhere – on the large old house he hadn't the courage to stop at, on the purse still weighing in his pocket like self-reproach – and he barely spoke. Then, after never more than a half-hour, he would get up and leave as brusquely as he'd arrived, taking up his ten-speed and going back down the road, not looking, with effort, at Sasha's house on his way home.

*

He didn't always just come to Cormic's. He did that only when his courage gave out at the last moment as he was coming to her house and he convinced himself that he'd meant to come to Cormic's after all, cycling on, to distract himself from his fear and his failure. There were other times, yes, when he did more than that, when he would loop slowly and unsteadily before her now-looming home, and twice had even gone so far as to have stopped before it with one foot planted on the broken pavement and his bike momentarily leaning against his clenched leg. Until, finally, one afternoon, without thinking beyond what he was doing at each moment he was doing it, his head down and his face fixed, he propped his bike against the Dovonovitches' broken fence and walked through their gate and up their wooden steps and rapped his fist on the rattling screen door. He took a step back and stood on the porch with the purse now in his hand, sweating despite the breeze, and tried to make himself look unafraid.

It was a Saturday. Sasha's mother appeared in her housedress, surprising him with her unkempt figure, her expressionless blue eyes. 'Yes?' she said.

'Is this yours?' Tom said, thrusting the purse at her.

'Yes, it is,' she said after a moment's inspection, without apparent interest or surprise.

'I found it at the end of the drive,' he blurted out.

She nodded. He could see Sasha's shoes in the hallway behind her and he took a deep breath, as though he were about to say something more. 'Thank you,' he said, nonsensically, then he suddenly turned without another word, strode back down their stairs, picked up his bike and rushed silently away.

*

Autumn came to Bear Lake late that year, and in November a relative mildness still lingered, before the shock of winter. The snows had not yet come, but it was nevertheless still bracing enough by Guy Fawkes Night for everyone to move closer to the bonfires crackling about town, sending up bursts of cinder. Scattered fires were lit in backyards across Bear Lake, fed by dried wood, boxes, long branches and all the old furniture that the town cleared itself of once a year, in varying conflagrations.

Cindy's sister was having a party in the back of their house, and Cindy had invited Cormic. They seemed to run into each other more often now, or at least took more notice of each other than they had before. She'd invited him to the party one afternoon when he was coming back from school and ran into her at the edge of her driveway at the end of the street.

'Hey Daly,' she cried sarcastically, referring to the store where he'd apparently bought the shirt he'd worn to the movies. 'My sis's having a bonfire party in a couple of weeks. Wanna come?

'I heard your friend went to Sasha's with her purse,' she went on, with evident disdain. 'That was really stupid! Her dad almost had a conniption! He didn't believe *your friend's* stupid lie about finding it at the end of the driveway like a pot of gold. Fucking idjit! So,' smiling, 'you coming to the party?'

Cormic mentioned nothing about it to Tom and brought along Denis instead, since Cindy had made it clear enough she didn't want Tom there, but even as they were walking down Elizabeth Street, having just passed the Dovonovitches' house on their right, where a yellow light lit the front room, Tom literally stepped from the shadows.

'You guys going to Cindy's?' he asked, innocently.

'You can't come, Tom. You're not invited,' Denis insisted.

Tom looked at him and said nothing and put his hands in his pockets and joined anyway.

Cindy met Tom with displeasure when they arrived and consequently hugged Cormic with pronounced enthusiasm. 'I'm so glad you came!' she cried, then waved her hand. 'Hi Denis.' She looked at Tom again and pointedly ignored him.

The whole backyard seemed ablaze, illuminating the trees further up the hill behind the house. Silhouettes moved against a huge bonfire, drinking and dancing, dragging branches and logs across the grass and taking them up in twos to hurl into the fire. The light flickered on the back of the house and its concrete steps, where more people sat. The boys didn't know anyone. A knot of wood popped in the flames and sent a couple dancing back into them laughing, then some people tossed more wood into the fire.

'Those are all my sis's friends,' Cindy said, pointing proudly, and, a little drunk, let her hand briefly rub against Cormic's when she dropped it.

Sasha was sitting on a log by the fire with her feet together and her hands between her knees, speaking with an older boy. He was leaning towards her, very drunk, with one hand on his knee and offering her a beer. She shook her head with an uncomfortable smile and continued to listen to him politely.

'You remember Sasha...' Cindy said to Tom, smiling.

Tom nodded without looking at her, his eyes transfixed on the log.

A couple burst from the shadows, stumbling, and pushed everyone aside.

'Where are your parents?' Denis asked, annoyed. 'Everyone's drinking!'

Cindy looked at him, incredulous, and laughed. 'They're inside,' she said, leading them through a jungle of shadows and silhouettes. 'They said my sis could have a party,' she shouted back. 'This is a party!' Steely Dan was playing loudly from a nearby ghetto blaster on the ground. 'C'mon,' she said, grabbing Cormic by the hand, and they passed beyond the fire to a cooler stashed further back among the trees. 'Make sure no one's looking,' she said, then took out three beers and handed them around. Denis opened his beer and sipped it suspiciously. Cindy tried to sit down and swayed against Cormic. 'Oops!' she suddenly said, laughing, holding a hand to her mouth, and pointed to where they could see her father standing before the fire, a pleasant-looking man with his hands behind his back, talking to some of his daughter's friends. Cindy smiled at Cormic and not long after said, 'You're cute,' then, drunker than she'd thought, fell down.

Tom hadn't joined them. He'd remained where they'd been, then eventually walked over and sat at the far end of the log where Sasha was talking to the other boy, and sat there for a long time, glancing over at her, then staring into the fire, frowning. Sasha glanced over once and saw him and looked almost frightened. The two sat, the fire snapping between them, with the voice of the third, the other boy, droning on. When finally it seemed like the older boy was not going to leave, Tom stood up and went over and said to her, interrupting the other boy, 'Hi.' It was right about this time that Denis said, 'I don't feel so well,' having finished his second beer by the cooler, and not long after that went home and got them all in trouble by vomiting on his mother's shoes.

Cindy watched Tom and Sasha and the other boy sitting on the log far back from the flickering light and shadows from the bonfire, with Tom on one end, and Sasha on the other, and the older boy between them. She watched the older boy turn, smiling, and shake Tom's hand, and Tom, impassive, shake his. Sasha sat, as though frozen. Embers rose in the night air and exploded. The older boy kept talking, reached into a cooler at his feet and offered a beer to Tom, who refused. Tom and Sasha glanced at each other awkwardly, timidly, while the older boy remained between them, talking, oblivious. Tom suddenly stood and moved closer to the fire, and Sasha watched him while still listening to the other boy. When the other boy finally rose to pee among the trees, Tom turned and walked back and sat beside Sasha on the log. They seemed to barely speak, then suddenly Sasha laughed, and Tom seemed to loosen, and even the older boy, when he returned, still doing up his fly, appeared to understand what was happening, and looked down at them drunkenly and shook his head and laughed. He picked up a last beer from the ground and offered it to Sasha, as some final gallant gesture, then stumbled away among the bouncing shadows and tinkling music and crackling flames.

Tom spoke, with his elbows on his knees. Sasha sat listening. Tom reached out once and lightly, unsurely, touched her knee. She seemed to stiffen, seemed even to move an inch away, and they were both silent again. There was no more laughing. The fire snapped between them. Then Sasha rose, for it was getting late, and found Cindy. 'Thank you, Cinds – Hi Cormic – I've got to go home,' she said, her face flustered, her eyes timid and warm. She walked back down the dark drive alone.

A few days later, Cindy organised a game of Kick-the-Can in her backyard with those who had been at the bonfire, including Tom. Later that evening, having hidden while Tom, the It, was meant to be seeking everyone out, Cindy came running around the corner of the house, racing against Cormic to strike home, laughing, when suddenly they both stopped, stunned, for there, at the back of the house, they found them – two small silhouettes, kissing each other awkwardly, as against the autumn wind.

'Hey Tom,' she called, angry. 'You're It!'

PART TWO

V

It began, for Sasha, well enough. She felt that her presence tempered his manner, which, in the beginning at least, inflated by his enthusiastic convictions and young pride, seemed at times almost belligerent. In certain moments, in the middle of some long discourse, he would glance at her accusingly, then smile, first at her, then, finally, at himself. Her modesty seemed to provide a sense of irony that he naturally lacked.

They met discreetly, for Sasha was not yet allowed to date: after school downtown, usually among friends; rarely, in public, alone. Once, in January, they planned a trip together to Corner Brook, where Sasha had organised to go shopping with Cindy. Tom and Cormic drove up in the car Tom had borrowed from his mother to meet them. They walked among the shops and ice statues of the Winter Carnival, holding hands for the first time openly, tentatively.

That first year passed, and Sasha, more than Tom, seemed to blossom. With Tom, it was more a general easing of his manner, a sort of loosening of the bolts with which he sealed up, harnessed and directed his innate drive. But with Sasha it was like watching a small flower open – hesitant, at first, then with delicate, unassuming pride. She laughed more, she grew her hair longer, and her eyes, though still shy, shone with more certain confidence.

'You should thank me for your good looks,' he told her.

'Don't be silly,' she said, laughing.

'You'll have to criticise my parents for that,' he said, which made her laugh again.

And then one day, when, after almost a year of dating, he'd brought her to the clearing by the log chute, something deep within her changed, irrevocably, and she felt, despite what she should have felt (what Cindy had told her, though how, really, could Cindy have known?), even a little sad.

They had gone by the chute when the winter had finally blown away, after the earth had thawed and the air softened. She'd walked beside him, quiet, while he'd led, nervous but pretending not to be, and unable to stop talking. 'Yeah, my brother was over last night with his girlfriend... The room beside me... I could barely sleep...' he said, glancing at her, and laughed nervously. 'You know, Cindy's always bragging about it, but it's no big deal,' he said again later, trying to be authoritative, but she'd only watched him, still quiet, and nodded. And so she'd followed him there that afternoon nonetheless, her hand in his, through the pollen-filled air, with him carrying the picnic (the ostensible reason for going there) and filling the silence with his endless words, until the moment it happened and she'd seized up and tried to show him, by a tremulous, calming smile, that it didn't hurt.

After, they'd walked back out in silence, hand in hand, more awkward than relieved, holding each other's hands because it was what they thought they should do. Dusk was deepening over the forest and they walked silently along the path through the trees that had led them there, onto the tracks that would lead them further out onto the resource road by the canal, running one way towards the mill and the other way back towards town. 'Are you okay?' he asked.

'Yes.' She nodded.

Then, awkwardly: 'Does it hurt?'

'I'm fine,' she told him, and hugged him to make him feel better.

Dusk had fallen by the time they got back. It was June, and the late summer evenings had not yet come. He left her with a kiss – a kiss that, on her side, was more certain now, less merely accepting than before. They parted at the top of Elizabeth Street, so that it might look like she was simply coming back from Cindy's house.

'I'll see you tomorrow,' he told her warmly, then stole a kiss again.

'Bye,' she said.

She walked back down Elizabeth Street alone after watching Tom making his way down the hill, slowly, as though relieved or confused. She stood for a long moment at the bottom of her front stairs looking up at their house, where light from the front room shone out through the fragrant dark, and everything else was still.

'Hi Mom,' she called when she got in, smiling now before anyone else could see. 'I'm home!'

*

In the summer of that second year, the logging industry fell. The rumours that had been circulating since the year before proved to be in part true, though the lay-offs were nowhere near as catastrophic as people like Mrs Ball had claimed they would be. 'They're stealing the soul, the very soul, from our poor little town. Oh, they'll make a ghost town of us yet!' she had declared, to herself and anyone else who would listen. But she had not been alone in her anxieties; others, too, had begun to despair of the town's future. So it came as a relief to Sasha when finally only a dozen or so men were laid off, as unfortunate as that fact was, while the great majority, including her father, were kept on with the same pay and the warning from the mill manager, 'We'll have to tighten our belts some, but for the moment, everything should be fine.'

The town then got on with life much as before, with those who had been laid off holed up in bars, exploding into fist fights every now and then, finding whatever job they could, and greeted with a sense of shame and embarrassment by most everyone else whose lives had not changed. One among those who had been laid off, Jamie Dence, or 'Dencey' as his high-school friends used to call him, caused more trouble than he was worth.

It was a Saturday now, midsummer. Main Street was busy with people coming in and out of Home Hardware, picking up orders from the Sears catalogue and strolling along between the shops, as Sasha and Cindy were doing then, arm in arm, on their way to get their hair cut. Jamie was leaning against the window of the pool hall smoking, his eyes hidden behind the cheap, oversized sunglasses he wore. He had been let go by the mill the month before, the first, having been hired out of high school three years earlier when the logging industry was still healthy. Not long after, the local mill and dam, both owned by the same company, were vandalised: graffiti was left at both locations, but at the dam the pump box had been angrily beaten and dented, and the windows of the valve house sprayed black. Everyone, including Sasha's father, had suspected Jamie but there was no proof, and he was either smart enough or satisfied enough to have left it at that.

His face now was lifted to the sunshine, stoutly expressionless, defiant in its apparent haughty indifference to what the passers-by might think, declaring his autonomy even from the pool hall itself by standing before its front window when everybody else gathered to smoke in the parking lot behind, hidden from view. He had been years above Sasha in school and she knew, as everyone knew, that he was much too old to be hanging out at the pool hall, where he was viewed by the kids, despite the cries of 'Hey Jamie' or 'Hey Dencey!', as something of a vague and troubling warning of what they too might become. They were almost embarrassed by him. He was like an isolated sign at the end of the road they were all on by skipping school, drinking and getting high, which showed that road's abrupt and desolate end. He was standing against the wall as they passed, his head dipped down, tired lines in the corners of his sunglasses, apparently looking at and thinking about nothing, when he seemed to see them and thinly smiled.

'Hey-hey,' he said, perhaps more for relief from boredom than anything else. Sasha and Cindy glanced at him, taken aback, stared quizzically, then kept on, still talking.

'What?' he barked after them, a sudden note of anger in his voice. 'You too good to talk to me?' He thrust down his cigarette and, in two strides, he was walking beside them.

'I was just asking your names,' he said now in a friendlier tone, following, not even looking ahead and even, in a moment of earnestness, taking off his glasses to reveal strikingly clear cyan-coloured eyes that sparkled with amusement and made him almost handsome.

The girls kept talking between themselves as he followed. 'Get lost!' Cindy finally said, but rather than making Jamie angry, it made him laugh. And perhaps because Sasha had said nothing at all, or because he sensed her uneasiness, or simply because she was the closest to him, between himself and the girl who had just told him to get lost and who seemed now merely to amuse him, he began to focus all his attention on her.

'What's your name?' he asked her, smiling as though he were talking to a child. Sasha, who had her head down, looked uneasily between Cindy and the ground, glanced once at Jamie and then, so as not to encourage him, looked as quickly away.

'Don't talk to him, Sasha,' Cindy said.

'Sasha,' Jamie said, smiling. 'That's a pretty name.'

The girls had quickened their steps. They reached the end of the sidewalk now, where it was cut by a side road before it continued towards the cinema. As though this was the limit of his territory, as it were, or his daytime comfort zone, although they'd only walked some 100 metres from the pool hall, Jamie slowed, then stopped. 'Bye Sasha!' he shouted and, as though proud of himself, stood smiling and watched them leave before heading back inside the pool hall, looking for friends.

Had it ended there, she might have forgotten all about it: no one would have talked, Jamie might have never been an issue. But it didn't. Any time he saw Sasha after that, he would whistle or wink, depending on where they were: when she passed him before the pool hall on her way downtown, when they saw each other on Main Street, once in the grocery mart, where he'd winked at her with a smile behind her mother's back. Once or twice, seeing her on the sidewalk, he called out 'Hey Sasha!' in a chipper tone, despite the others around them and taking obvious delight in that fact. It got to the point where she avoided walking by the pool hall to go downtown and instead walked the longer way down, past the public elementary school and corner store along the far side of the hill, past the tiny police station and the now-abandoned railhouse so that she joined Main Street on the opposite end, by the hotel and the cinema. At first, when he began eyeing her, she'd been uncomfortable, then uneasy, which only seemed to encourage him. Then finally one day, when he appeared to have found out her full name and where she lived, she grew fearful.

'Hey-hey, Sasha,' he said, appearing one day in his car as she was walking home alone uphill after she'd crossed the railroad tracks, his car moving slowly beside her. She tried not to hurry or look at him. 'What are you up to?' he said. 'Hey, you still not talking to me? Hey... Hey, how's the old man?' at which she suddenly, for the first time, looked at him, startled that he knew that much, while he sat, one hand over the wheel, the other cocked outside the window, driving up the wrong side of the road.

'He used to be my boss, old Jack, your "Pappy".' He laughed. 'You still not gonna talk to me? I'm putting a lot of effort into this. I'm not a bad guy. You're really pretty, you know that? No joke. You gonna at least look at me? Why don't you look at me? — Hey!' he snapped. 'Look at me!' She looked at him, obedient, scared it could go further. 'You see, I ain't so bad… You sure are pretty…'

Sasha continued up the hill, faster. He stopped just before her street and turned his car around and headed back down as she continued on alone, forcing herself not to run or look back, waiting until she was in her room before she even really let herself feel the entirety of the fear rise like wild horses within her. And it was only then, when she felt scared enough, that she said something to Tom about it, and to Tom alone. Not for him to do something – no, no, she didn't want that – but only because, she felt, even angry with him as she spoke, he'd almost forced her to.

*

Tom had noticed something wrong with Sasha in the weeks before but he hadn't known what it was exactly. With another school year under way, he had mostly been absorbed in his studies, for he had the discipline of mind and the kind of brutality of spirit that allowed him to push all other preoccupations from his thoughts. This included, for the most part, thoughts of Sasha, which came to him only when he let his hand fall from his head to his desk and looked into space for a moment before absorbing himself in his work again. But he had noticed recently that something was bothering her, and it troubled him. She seemed quieter, preoccupied, more withdrawn than usual when they met. 'Is everything okay?' he'd asked her on two different occasions, to which she'd replied, without even trying to pretend to look surprised at the question, 'Yes... Yes,' and forced herself to smile. He hadn't pushed the subject further, not because he wasn't interested but because he didn't know what else to do. Then the day came when the trouble quivering at the back of her eyes, which she usually tried to eclipse with a smile, covered her whole face; she was pale, her whole mien was dim, and she barely spoke to him. They were walking in silence in the woods by her house, remaining discreet even though their relationship was an open secret to everyone but the parents, when he finally stopped her.

'Are you sure everything's okay?' he asked, believing the problem might have something to do with them. She looked down, and for a moment it looked like she was going to weep, but she didn't. 'Some man keeps bothering me...' she told him, her eyes on the ground, even a little ashamed, and, for the first time in his life, he felt his blood freeze.

'What man?'

'Some man downtown.'

'Why didn't you tell me before?'

'Because I didn't want to,' she said obdurately, a little defiantly.

'Have you told your dad?'

'No.'

'Who have you told?'

'No one.'

'Why not, Sasha?!'

'Because I didn't think it was a problem,' she almost shouted.

He looked at her, confused and angry. 'What's his name?'

'It doesn't matter.'

'Then why are you telling me?'

'Because you asked!' she yelled at him. They had stopped in the middle of a path among the trees. He stared at her, frustrated, not knowing what to do, though he knew, despite himself, that forcing the issue would only push her further into silence. It was perhaps best, he thought, to let it be.

'He followed me home Saturday...'

Tom appeared in the bar Thursday of the following week. He had said nothing about his thoughts, not even that day Sasha had told him everything, as he walked her to the end of her street, then walked back home, alone. At school, he seemed more preoccupied than usual; was silent and morose.

'Hey man, you okay? What's up?' Cormic asked one day on the school grounds and he had looked up with annoyance, even disdain, levelling the apparent flippancy of the question.

'Nothing,' he eventually said, then changed the subject, frowning: 'You want to race?'

The bar was near empty the day he entered. It was still early, and there were four men sitting at the bar. It lay just off Main Street, one of a handful in town, a small and derelict place but the most popular among the loggers, and it had the air, in the early evening – with the dusk pressing on the lit windows and the lingering odour of stale sweat – of lonely expectation. Stray woodchips that had collected over years lay wedged in the corners. Jamie hadn't even seen Sasha that week; he appeared to have grown tired of the whole thing, or had simply forgotten about it. Like the other three men beside him, he turned around at the sound of the front door opening, then looked away again. He was the youngest there, and the loudest. Tom remained where he was, just inside the front door, until the men stopped talking and looked back at him again. Then he looked directly at Jamie, the third man in, and said: 'Stop talking to my girlfriend.'

Jamie stared at him, with no idea of who he was. 'Who's your— Sasha?' he asked, then smiled. He looked Tom up and down – saw the naked fear, the flushed cheeks – and laughed good-naturedly. The others looked at Tom too and smiled. 'C'mon, let me buy you a drink,' Jamie said, after the incredulous pause. 'What's your name? Bud, can I buy him a beer? No? How about a soda?' he said, turning again to Tom. 'I didn't mean no harm.'

'Stop talking to her. Leave her alone. You're scaring her,' Tom said.

'I didn't mean to scare nobody. Hey-hey, c'mon,' Jamie said, putting his arm around Tom's shoulder and leading him to the bar. 'Hell, I didn't even know she had a boyfriend. She said nothing to me about it,' he continued, wryly. They were standing at the counter now, with Tom, still frowning, looking at him uncertainly.

'That's Mia's boy,' the bartender said, but Tom ignored it.

'You're her boyfriend?' Jamie said, delighted. 'You sure is lucky. She's a pretty thing. How is she, eh, eh? You must be having a good time, eh, eh?' he said, laughing again his too-loud laughter, and slapping Tom on the shoulder. 'I'm just joking! Here, have your soda. I'll get you a beer another time. It ain't legal here and I wouldn't want to get my friend Bud in trouble, right Bud? You work out?' he continued ceaselessly, taking Tom by the arm. 'You're big there for a fourteen-year-old. How old are you, fourteen? Yep, that's right about the age I started though not with a girl as pretty as Sasha.'

'Jamie, why don't you let the kid alone,' said one of the other men at the bar.

'Let him alone? Hey, I'm just being friends,' he said, turning to Tom. 'She never told me she had a boyfriend all the times I talked to her. I was just having fun. I didn't mean no harm by it. Right?'

63

'Leave her alone,' Tom made himself say again, with less conviction than before.

'Sure I'll leave her alone. Wouldn't want to mess with these,' he said, holding Tom's arm again and laughing.

'Stop being an ass, Jamie,' another man at the bar said, uncomfortable.

'I'm not being an ass. I'm just trying to make the kid feel good. C'mon,' he said to Tom, 'I'll walk you out. Are we friends? Cool, eh?' He reached into his pocket for his wallet but Tom refused the offer and tried to pay.

'It's on the house,' the bartender told him, frowning, while Tom walked now with Jamie towards the front door and Jamie raised his arm and put it around Tom's shoulder, still talking and laughing. They walked that way together, side by side, to the door until it opened out onto where the dusk light was mingling with the dark and the cool smell of the evergreens hung on the air and the light from the window of the bar fell on the ground beside the two wooden steps they now passed down, with the door whapping closed behind them and silence following like a fist. And as though upon the whapping of the door, on the tail end of a laugh that hung in the air like something half-abandoned, disengaged from the thoughts that were already elsewhere, Jamie tripped Tom on the last step. He fell upon him furiously, his long hair swinging before his eyes until it grew matted with sweat, his arm under the old lumber jacket he still wore rising and falling in an unbroken hook even after Tom was curled up on the ground bleeding, not even struggling anymore, until he stopped suddenly and looked at Tom with his arm still raised as though he might strike again, breathing harshly and unevenly, as though filled with fear at himself, and said, 'Don't ever fucking come back here again.'

Afterwards, inside, everyone said, Jamie's eyes remained dark. 'Give me a beer,' he said, once he had retaken his stool, waiting until he'd taken a drink and his hand had stopped trembling before he looked up and smiled, then finally began to laugh, while the other men looked away.

VI

Winter came in strong and cold, in endless sheets of snow that fell dizzy and multifarious among the deciduous and evergreens, blanketing the streets and yards and houses in drifts that mounted so high sometimes overnight that families would have to send a child out a window to shovel a path from their screen door, if they wanted to be sure to get out of their homes at all. There were days the flurries were so bad that you couldn't see your hand before your face, but when they settled, the sun came out solid and bright, the sky shone as blue as the sea and the whole town, in utter stillness, with few people yet venturing outdoors, seemed sequestered by a kind of bright silence – still and radiant, with, here and there, the flapping of a bird flying up from a branch, the thump of snow falling upon the ground below.

It was the happiest Tom and Sasha had ever been. Tom's incident with Jamie Dence had become the past, and had even brought more good than bad. He had hobbled for a while from pain, with bruises along his back and shoulder, but there was nothing broken and little obvious except a black scar where his lip had been split, which he'd been unable to hide. 'Who did this to you? What happened? What brute? What brute?!' his mother had cried the next morning when he emerged for breakfast, shame-faced; but he'd kept still in his chair, looking down at the table and at the breakfast she'd laid out for him. Still in her dressing gown, her hair unkempt, she hung over him until he, still looking down, answered with a sullen and obstinate, 'No one.'

'No one!' his mother cried, in their great empty house, nestled into the side of the hill like something that neither Nature nor Love nor Time could ever remove, despite, or because of, the husband who had left her and the older sons who had gone (the oldest, who was lumbering up north and never came home; the other, who, in a travelling rock band, came home once in a while and played in the town rink to the cheers of the kids who saw him as a local hero but who, in reality, lived out of his van); set there, like the mother, with a kind of unremitting and sorrowful hauteur.

'I fell off my bike,' Tom told her, looking up at her, and would say no more. She'd looked at him, shocked, and even, it seemed to him, hurt.

'You do what you like, son,' she told him coldly, and left him to eat in the kitchen alone.

But if he'd said nothing about it to his mother or, for that matter, anyone else, Mr Dovonovitch must have heard about it from the other men, for he appeared in the bar not long after. 'We're going to talk,' he told Jamie. They went outside, and though no one exactly knew what he said, Jamie wasn't seen or heard from again for a long time (some said that, having declared that there was nothing left in this 'shithole' of a town, he'd gone north seeking more work). And where Tom once only dared to walk Sasha to the end of her street, he was now able to walk her all the way home. It was as if, after the beating he'd taken from Jamie, and Mr Dovonovitch's words with Jamie following that, there was no need to pretend anymore. He'd passed Mr Dovonovitch downtown and felt that old dread, that old fear, seize him, when he saw her father look at him and, frowning, nod; and then one eve, after he'd dared walk her to the end of the drive again, there Mr Dovonovitch stood, at the top of the front stairs, as if to show he knew, but said nothing still.

'Does it still hurt?' Sasha asked him once, concerned.

'I'm okay,' he told her, prouder than he'd ever been before.

He had even once now been left with her in their front room, when the mother was out shopping and the father had had to go. 'You be careful,' the father told Sasha, glancing at Tom as he might have glanced at a useless lamp. 'Okay,' Sasha said and even as they sat listening to her father leave, with Tom still hardly daring to move, she reached across the couch and silently took his hand in hers.

*

That same winter, Denis Brichard died in an accident, against which none raised their fists at the heavens or, for the most part, pointed fingers of blame; they accepted it with a sort of austere general silence, in respect for his grieving family. 'His mother shouldn't ha' been letting him play in that thing like that alone,' some dared say, but it was said quietly, in a tone of regretful truth, at which most just nodded, accepting the death in the same way they accepted the accidental death of a lumberer in the woods or a relative at sea, capsized and drowned. Tom and the others accepted the news in much the same manner, not from any inherited stoicism, but because they hadn't really known Denis well. They'd never really seen him much beyond the brief interlude that first summer when Tom had gone to his house more and more in order to see Sasha. His absence, by death, was no different really than his usual absence, except that the news briefly dimmed the winter festivities and made the days that eventually followed feel, strangely, more festive, as though they'd all stepped from beneath some enormous shadow.

Rumours of Denis's death made the rounds in the homeroom the day after it happened, though most people were only vaguely aware of who Denis was.

'Jesus, what happened?' Cormic ran up to Tom at break.

'Didn't your father tell you?' he said, shortly, almost annoyed. 'He suffocated. A tunnel in his snow-fort fell in on him, and he couldn't get out. A chunk of ice probably knocked him on the back of the head anyways. Maybe he wasn't awake. His mom found him when he didn't come in to dinner.'

'Jesus…'

'They're not going to be letting forts round here for a while,' Tom said, and while he went to the service like everyone else, that was all he ever said aloud, even though, all things considered, he'd probably known Denis better than anyone from the hours he'd spent at his house that summer, waiting to catch a glimpse of Sasha. And he was right – there were no more snow-forts built that year, or at least not on the scale that Denis used to make them, those castles built up from snow-banks at the end of his drive, with separate rooms and windows, iced with water, and, Tom remembered, having even a little dungeon-like room buried deep down, where you'd slide to the bottom and try to scramble back up again. These were things Denis worked at every winter with the same childish pride with which he'd built his BMX engine or the haunted houses he used to fashion in his basement for Halloween, when they were very young and visited out of boredom. Poor Denis, Tom thought. He'd been a smart boy, smarter than anyone gave him credit for. He remembered him as an always marginal figure, happily working away at his own projects by himself, oblivious to what others thought: and then one day, he was gone... The unfinished snow-fort he left at the end of his drive remained there for days after his death like some glacial sepulchre until one morning that too, like Denis, was gone, smashed to bits overnight by his outraged mother or father, its ice foundations still rising jagged in the morning sunlight.

*

'That is life,' Sasha's father told her. 'Hand me the saw.' They were in the woodshed below the house, chopping logs in the early dark, the air inside comforting with the smell of resin and packed wood, the dark and snow outside the woodshed's open door smelling cold and empty. There was a naked bulb on, bright above them, which her father had fashioned there, makeshift, as he had fashioned the woodshed below the kitchen, out of plywood – not to keep the warm in but to keep the snows out. There were lines of logs on either side that they used to heat the house and at the end her father's tools, some hanging on nails, some scattered among debris and woodchips on the earthen floor. The place was cool in the summer, but very cold in winter. She got the saw from the ground by the wall, and brought it to him. His work lumber jacket was off and he stood, sweating in the cold, in a dirty sleeveless shirt, over a pile of logs he'd chopped into smaller bits. His wet, spiked hair shone beneath the bulb's light.

She handed him the handsaw. He studied her for a moment, then handed it back. 'Cut the kindling,' he said, and left her to saw off the small branches and throw them in a pile by the door, through which he now passed, his boots thumping heavily up the back steps, then on the kitchen floor above. Sasha cut the branches off and chopped more kindling from the logs he'd left until her shirt was damp beneath her winter jacket, then she put the saw back up on a nail on the back wall, and went back outside through the dark and snow – leaving the light on, for they always left the light on – and up the stairs to the kitchen. Her father was sitting at the table, a new shirt on now, reading the paper spread before his enormous figure, the kitchen reflected in the window behind him. When she entered he tipped the paper down and stared at her to see if she was better now, then folded the paper up again.

'Here you go, love,' her mother said, and put a grilled cheese sandwich and glass of milk on the table before her, then sat and ate the same in silence.

Sasha, who had grown up across the street from Denis, was more affected by what had happened than any of them. It visibly upset her when she passed the Brichards' dark and silent front door – no more dark or silent than it had been before, but seeming to her now to be shut against or closing in the memory of that strange boy she used to see playing before it her whole life. It played on her mind and called up fears from deep within, rising like fumes, shuddering the repose on her face. When returning home and turning in to her front drive alone, she tried not to look at the house, tried not to hurry but hurried nonetheless, feeling behind her that door, that house, as some cold, implacable space hurrying her into the heavy heat of her own home and its brightly lit rooms, with her father in the woodshed below, the distant sound of her mother in the kitchen and the dog barking at nothing in the backyard. 'Mom,' she called. 'Do you need me to do anything?'

'I'm okay.' Her mother smiled, blandly.

'Can I help you in the kitchen?' she said, eager to do something, to move.

'Just do your homework, dear,' her mother said kindly, oblivious, and Sasha's face faltered. 'Are you okay?' her mother asked her once, with dim apprehension of something not quite right, emerging from the kitchen in the inevitable housedress and bearing a tray of food to her sister's room. Sasha nodded, not wanting to worry her. 'Yes,' she said, and her mother smiled a perfunctory smile, then carried on into her sister's room.

'I hope Denis's parents are okay,' she said to Tom later that day.

He had his arm around her and nodded and pulled her closer.

'I wonder if it hurt him...'

'It's okay, Sash. He's in heaven now.'

'How do you know he's in heaven?'

'I don't know for sure, but I think he is.'

'Maybe there's no heaven,' she ventured.

Tom frowned. 'I think there is,' he said.

'How do you know?'

'What do you mean, how do I know?' he said impatiently. 'I don't know for certain. I just believe there is. You think all this comes from nothing?'

'But you don't know for certain, Tom. You don't!'

'Don't be foolish, Sasha,' he said, in a more comforting tone.

She was silent for a long while, then said. 'I just hope his parents are okay...'

*

These dark moments passed, however, and with Denis's service over and the town's respectful quiet lifted – though Denis's front door remained perpetually closed, the house sunk in mournful silence – they organised a ski trip a couple of weekends later in order to get away. The snow had been falling daily since the week before the trip, as though to bury that most recent past, and the four of them piled into Cindy's car on a bright and cloudless Saturday, to drive some forty-five minutes away to the basic ski station built into the side of a mountain outside Corner Brook.

Memories of Jamie seemed far away, as did those of Denis, as did anything that could impinge upon the bright freedom of a moment set in relief against the recent tragedy of Denis's death. Tom, sitting in the backseat with Sasha beneath a blanket, seemed in especially high spirits.

'Stop it...' Sasha said, pushing his hands away from her beneath the blanket. 'Tom, stop it!' she said stoutly. He moved away, then suddenly kissed her on the cheek, which made her shake her head at him and, despite herself, smile.

'Can you roll down your window,' he called to Cindy, who was driving. 'Your cigarette's killing me.'

'It's my car,' Cindy told him. 'Roll down your own.' He was in too good spirits to be annoyed, as he might have been on another occasion, and rolled down his window as Cindy told him to. A few moments later, Cindy glanced at him in the rear-view mirror and rolled down her window, too.

'You're a real pain, you know that?' she said.

'Cormic,' he called, 'can you tell her I can't hear her?', which made Sasha laugh and Cindy shake her head and Cormic, beside her in the front seat, laugh too.

They drove along the highway with the river opening up beside them on one side and trees rising up higher along the hills on the other. The road twisted and rose and lost the river, then fell and followed it again; the trees gave way to cliffs, then rose among the foothills leading up to Corner Brook. The ski hill lay about twenty minutes outside the town and was packed. Sun blazed over the small slopes and the maze of figures making their way down them, slowly and widely on the lower slopes, quicker among the higher ones. Sasha rarely skied, so they started on the bunny slope, among the cries of children and occasional clattering of skis. She was unsteady at first, but Tom skied beside her, guiding, proud, excited for her. 'Good Sash, good,' he said, slowly moving beside her. 'Good. Now turn, turn.'

'I'm turning!' she exclaimed, scared and annoyed.

'Okay, Sasha, just turn a little more. Move with your arms. Like this,' he said, and flailed his arms like he was having a fit.

'Ha ha,' she said, though it calmed her and made her forget her fear for a moment.

Her eyes glittered with the cold and sunlight and her cheeks were stung red from the cold; she was happy. He whipped beside her too close once, recklessly, and almost made her fall, then swung out further and stopped to make sure she was okay. 'Stop showing off, Tom!' she said, but it was clear, nonetheless, that she was proud of him.

The sun shone high and began to melt the snow and it was so bright now it smarted their eyes. For lunch they ate sloppy joes and drank pop in the small restaurant by the parking lot. The town felt far away. Sasha and Tom, their gloves off, their jackets opened in the acrid cafeteria heat, held hands on the bench almost unconsciously now. It didn't matter who saw them anymore.

'Let's go to a higher slope,' Tom suggested at lunch.

Cindy glanced at Sasha uncertainly and declared: 'I'm fine where we are.'

'I'd like to do some moguls,' he said, ignoring her. 'Do you wanna do some moguls?' he asked Cormic.

'Sure!'

'I'm going to stay here for the moment,' Sasha told him.

'C'mon Sash, it'll be fun, we can try it!'

'We're going to stay down here,' Cindy told him, angry now, collecting her tray and standing up, while Sasha, hesitant, still remained beside Tom.

'What are you worrying about, Cindy?' he snapped. 'She'll be fine.'

'I can make up my own mind!' Sasha said, also annoyed. All four of them had red lips from the sloppy joes.

'Fine!' Tom said.

'Fine!' Sasha said.

'Fine!' Cindy said.

'Okay,' Cormic said. 'I'm fine with whatever.'

They stayed on the easier slopes until a few runs later Tom, after much cajoling, convinced Sasha to turn right off the chairlift, instead of left, as they should have done, towards the easier runs they had been taking all day. 'We're going this way,' he called back when Cindy and Cormic arrived on the chairlift behind them, and pointed towards a slope that led to another chairlift that would take them further up. It was long past noon now and the moguls were high and set far apart, and the snow had melted heavy beneath the sun.

Sasha stood at the sharp edge of the slope.

'You sure I can do this…?'

'I'm sure you can,' Tom said. 'Just follow me,' and went off, the first to go down, slowly at first, then faster, and the others followed. Sasha remained leaning forward, the lengthening rays of the sun gentle on her cheeks, a colder breeze stirring the high smell of the trees, the cries of the bunny hill gone now and no one else there but a lone skier reaching the bottom below them, then pulling further away.

They had gone some way down before they noticed she was missing.

'C'mon Sash!' Tom called to where she remained above. 'C'mon.'

'I can't…'

'C'mon!!' he cried, encouraging.

'I can't!'

'I'll catch you!'

'You can't catch me…' She snorted, incredulous.

'Of course I'll catch you,' he shouted up to her. 'I promise.'

After a moment's hesitation, glancing at Tom and then seeming to look within herself, Sasha began to move down the hill, her body stiff with fear, her skis sloped inwards, looking as though something outside of her was pulling her, coming first to one mogul, then stopping, turning slowly and unsteadily and coming to another, again with that look that something was pulling her downwards.

'Good,' Tom said. 'Good.'

She kept coming. Faster and faster, then faster still, her arms opening in alarm, her eyes widening, her back broadening, before Tom realised, too late, she wasn't going to stop.

She hit him straight on. There was a loud clattering of skis and the two tumbled down the slope.

'I told you I'd catch you,' Tom mumbled, covered in snow. Spontaneously, surprising everyone there, Sasha suddenly kissed him on his reddened cheek and began to laugh: 'I know!'

That was the best memory of the day. Or, perhaps even better – when they were making their way home later that same evening in tired silence, and Sasha and Tom sat in the backseat again beneath the blanket, while Tom stared out at the passing lights and Sasha lay with her head on his shoulder, her eyes softly closed, as winds rattled at the windows like ghosts they had all, as yet, refused to let in.

VII

'Jamie Dence is back,' her father said one evening, speaking to her mother at the kitchen table. He looked at Sasha and said nothing, then took a bite of his steak, slowly finished it and looked again at her mother. 'Joe Walsh told me.'

Jamie, it turned out, hadn't gone too far north. He had, in fact, the town said, gone up to the capital for a while, looking for work and drinking away what money he had before returning to Bear Lake, burdened with rage against the world in general and against the town in particular. He'd walked back to Bud's with a stiff air and pulled up his usual stool as though he'd never left, sitting at the bar silently, his hair longer, his eyes dark with discontent, eventually forgetting himself and slouching as he drank.

'You back, Jamie?' the bartender asked.

There was no one else in the bar.

Jamie drank.

'Yeah,' he finally said, wiping his lips.

He lifted his eyes. 'So what's going on in this shithole?'

'Same old,' said the bartender.

Jamie looked at him, then nodded. He finished his beer and, considering another, held out a handful of coins in his palm, counted them up, saw there wasn't enough, and slapped all of them on the counter with disgust before leaving again.

People saw him then about town, more solitary than before, and drinking more. He wasn't working, and no one knew where he got the money to drink, for it was certainly more than unemployment could allow. It was said that he was living at home again with his father, an old house-ridden man no one had seen in public for years, in a house that reeked of poverty and mould, where Jamie slept in his old bedroom in the basement, for free.

'That's what Joe said,' Sasha's father told her mother, then wiped his lips, threw down his napkin and went into the living room to watch TV. Sometime later he went into the bar and saw Jamie, who glowered at Mr Dovonovitch and retreated into a corner, where he remained, alone, until Mr Dovonovitch finally seemed to forget Jamie was even there.

Sasha ran into him in line at the grocery mart downtown, taking a sharp breath upon seeing him, but his eyes only flicked over her, then flicked away again. He stared ahead without interest, and eventually took his bag of food and left without looking back, skulking through the front doors, then turning left and walking stiffly along the front window, with his single bag of food, against the dismal winter sky. But nothing happened beyond that, and everyone soon grew used to seeing him around. He never spoke to Tom or Sasha. He took to drinking as regularly, by himself, as before.

In any case, there were graver concerns. The lay-offs that had hit Bear Lake had happened across the island, and wildcat strikes had begun, fomented by an American communist who had come up from New England with the North American Loggers Union and who was hailed, despite his young age, as a great leader, on both the island and abroad. Years of long toil and low wages had fed into a simmering social rage, and this, coupled with the lay-offs, insecurity and declining wages, had created communities ready, like small patches of dry brush, to be set ablaze. Suddenly, they were hearing about union meetings in isolated hamlets, negotiations with management representatives, further lay-offs and growing unrest. But for Sasha and the others these still remained 'newspaper events', articles in the local paper that none of them, except Tom once in a while, ever read. Bear Lake, so far, remained calm, and their own daily concerns made the labour disputes seem distant, as if taking place in another world. One day, Mrs Ball sat down in Cormic's mother's kitchen and said: 'They're striking now in Huntstown' – drinking her tea – 'Sure, isn't it their right? The Lord knows they've been paying us a pittance for generations. My own father could hardly afford to house us, and him slaving his hours away out there in the sleet and snow. It's true we didn't have the chance to complain much then, happy with what we got we were, with those men in Corner Brook growing fat off us breaking our backs. But the time has come now; we're simply not willing to accept that anymore... And can you blame us? To think they're laying off those poor, poor workers, for their own greedy pockets... It's a sin, dear, a sin, to watch other men slowly while away their lives doing nothing... Who do they think they are, now, coming to our island and taking the food from our mouths! Ah, there'll be a price to pay... There always is, dear, there always is... Would you have a biscuit?' – and Cormic told Tom, who told Sasha, but they spoke nothing more of it beyond that.

The unrest finally came to Bear Lake at the town hall. More lay-offs had taken place, and the men had gathered for a meeting set up by executives from Corner Brook who, in turn, were responsible to the board. The room was filled with men who had been laid off and men who hadn't, many holding leaflets distributed by the more militant unions. Sasha went with Tom to see, and lingered in the front hall, trying to get a look in. 'What are you doing here? This is not a place for kids,' one of the St Clair teachers, upon seeing them, barked. 'We're watching,' Tom told her stoutly, and refused to leave. They snuck in the front door and stood at the back, behind a wall of angry and anxious workers and their wives. Mr Dovonovitch, as mill foreman, was sitting at the table at the front of the hall with a local union representative and one of two expected executives. He sat at the far end silently, a dark look on his face. The second executive finally entered and took the middle seat. He had a kind, ruddy face and an open, dignified air. He tapped his paper on the table and looked out for a moment at the men gathered, now silent, before him. 'Well then,' he said. 'Let's begin.'

The first man stood, a large fellow in his fifties who had been working the forests since he'd been a teenager. 'We'd like to know how many men you're planning on laying off,' he said.

'Yeahs' erupted around the room. Heads nodded.

'There'll be no more lay-offs in the immediate future, gentlemen,' the executive said. 'Thus far, we've done only what we had to do. It's been no more pleasurable for us than it has been for you, or anybody else. The industry is changing, as I'm sure you're all aware, and we've only made the adjustments we deemed necessary so the majority of us – of us all – could keep our jobs. I include myself in that. I've worked the forests too, just like you.'

'Then why aren't we getting more money?' someone shouted from the back, and there was more loud agreement.

'That isn't possible right now, but we're in negotiations,' he said.

'And what about the restructuring?'

'Some concessions will have to be made for that, but no one's anticipating any more lay-offs,' he said.

'What are ye at!?' someone shouted.

'How can we trust ye on that?' another cried.

'You have my word,' he said. 'I know how diffi-cult this it. It is not easy. We are taking things step by step for, as I've tried to point out, the greater benefit of all. I love this town. I know many people here,' he said, and gestured at Mr Dovonovitch and the crowd. 'Some economies were inevitable. We have done everything to make this as painless as possible – for you, for us, for everyone. The world is changing, and we need to change with it. It is the only way that we – and you, gentlemen,' he said, then nodded to many of the women, 'ladies, will survive.'

There were angry exclamations and more ques-tions, but little more, really, came from it than that. Eventually, everyone filed out. Sasha was outside with Tom, among a crowd waiting anxiously for a response, when Mr Dovonovitch emerged, his face heavy, and saw them. 'Sasha, get home,' he barked.

'Dad, I—'

'I told you to get home,' he snapped, and Sasha, startled, bowed her head obediently. Tom walked her back up the hill. It was a clear summer night. The street was empty, with everyone downtown, and they walked alone in the silence. Tom put his arm around her. 'We're going to get out of here,' he told her.

'Yeah,' she said quietly, and smiled for him, but like she didn't really believe it.

Cormic's family were already getting ready to leave before that, and were just waiting for school to finish up. They had been in Bear Lake for five years now and the decision to move had as much to do with his father's career path as with what his parents saw as the larger horizons for their children on the mainland.

They hosted a goodbye party at their house, including a number of kids from school. His parents were in a happy mood, the adults and kids mixed easily and the atmosphere, despite the recent worries, was festive. They'd made punch – one for adults, one for children – and the living room and kitchen were full of guests coming and going to say goodbye. Many brought gifts. 'You shouldn't have,' his mother said. 'We'll miss you,' they said. Tom and Sasha showed up in the early afternoon. He hadn't spent much time with either of them for months, since they now spent most of their time together alone, and the decision to move, which had only been sprung on him by his parents recently, had come as something of a surprise to them as much as Cormic.

'So, you leaving?' Tom said.

'Yeah.'

'Lucky bastard,' he said.

'Yeah,' Cormic said, but he felt sad.

Sasha, the last time he ever saw her, looked more

beautiful than she ever had. Tom stood with his arm around her proudly (her parents had not come, and it was not clear they had been invited) and although she was still only sixteen, she glowed with the gentle satisfaction, the sort of appreciative tranquillity, of a woman well loved.

'Where are you going?' she asked Cormic.

'We're going to Toronto.'

'It must be nice.'

'We'll go visit,' Tom told her. 'I want to go to med school there,' he told Cormic. He shook Sasha. 'We'll be getting out of this place soon enough.'

Sasha looked at him and smiled, not with indulgence really, or even hope, but with something like pride, and belief, at least, in him.

Cindy had been milling with the adults and came over now, carrying a cup of spiked drink she'd snuck from the adults' punch bowl.

'Leaving so soon?' she said, nudging Cormic.

'Gotta go,' he joked.

'Well, we'll miss you, to be honest. I may come visit! Hey, wouldn't that be cool, Sasha? We could go visit him. We could even let Tom come, if he's good.' She laughed, a little drunk.

Tom looked annoyed but tried to smile.

Sasha and Tom soon left. 'Bye,' Tom said, shaking his hand. 'Bye Cormic,' Sasha said, and gently hugged him. Cindy followed not long after. 'Bye Daly!' She laughed, then surprised him by kissing him frankly on the lips. 'Ha ha,' she cried and waved, stumbling a little down the steps. Later, he stood on the front steps and watched as the last of his parents' friends pulled from the drive and drove home unsteadily and the streetlights flickered on overhead, following the dip of the street, like stars.

*

Cormic and his family had been gone for seven weeks when it happened, and they only heard about it because someone from the town called. He was sitting in their new living room in Toronto watching football with his father when the phone rang and he heard his mother say, 'Yes... How are you?... Good, good... My God, is everyone okay?... What happened?' She eventually hung up and came into the living room and told them, 'There's been an accident in Bear Lake.' The exact details never made it into the papers. It was briefly mentioned with news in a mid-page article about the riots in Huntstown, during which a policeman had been killed, though it was never found out by whom, either because, as was said, silence was being kept by the community or because no one really knew for sure who did it. The events at the Bear Lake lumber mill were an addendum to this, an illustration of the further unrest happening around that time – before, that is, the whole movement petered out and things were settled, as best as they could be, for the logging industry.

PART THREE

VIII

Cindy was downtown when she heard the explosion, like the sky was the stretched skin of some distant drum and someone had struck a fist against it. It was a dull thumping, and for a moment, she wondered if she'd really heard it. The day was hot and heavy, late August, and people on Main Street, upon that muffled thump, stopped and turned and looked up and over towards where they thought they'd heard it from, then looked at each other, wondering, some worried, as if they knew already what might have been done, then looked back up again, into the merciless sun.

She had just come out of Sears, buying new clothes for school, and she stood there on the sidewalk, holding her bag – her new blouse, her new jeans, her new lipstick.

'Did you hear that?' someone asked.

'What was that?' another person said.

All along Main Street, more people had stopped, looking up, then others walking by, who perhaps had not heard it, spoke to them and looked up too, until all along the sidewalk it seemed everyone and everything had stopped. Cindy felt a vague dread.

'I think it's out by the mill,' she heard someone say. She squinted out that way, heard murmurs about her rise into an uneasy chorus of concern, then out on the blue, over the trees, they saw a thin stream of smoke rise slowly through the breathless air and stay for a moment, as if it were taunting them, unmoving.

*

As Cindy stood on the sidewalk, looking in the direction of a sound she was still not sure she had heard, Sasha separated herself from Tom and, having heard the explosion like a quick pop in the air, sat up with alarm. They were out in the woods, in the spot by the chute where they went to be alone. Shadows from the pine and spruce trees hung over them and the soft, warm ground.

'Did you hear that?'

'What?' Tom said lazily, still lying on the ground, his hand on her arm.

'Something exploded.'

'I didn't hear anything… Come on… Come back here…' he said, gently pulling her down.

She had a look now of mounting worry and pulled her arm from his. There was no other sound, except for the lazy drone of flies in the shadow of the woods and the snapping metal of the chute under the sun. Tom leaned up on an elbow, watching her listen with a look on her face of growing concern.

'It was probably just something at the mill,' he said.

'My dad's at the mill,' she said, and it came from her like a reproach. It was like she already knew. Her face was worried, and her voice trembled slightly; stray pine needles hung from her hair. Her father was there, she knew it, there was something wrong. That wasn't an ordinary sound. It was a sound she'd never heard before. But today was a Saturday – maybe he wasn't there, certainly he should be at home, in the woodshed or sitting in the living room with the paper while her mom cleaned and cooked and looked after everything, tended to her sister, while he sat... yes, he was sitting at home, a heavy, silent presence, certainly at home, not there, at the mill, from where the explosion had come like an interruption into their silence of some senseless language. She scrambled up. It was like Tom was no longer there as she started out ahead through the trees, walking briskly, trying not to run, as if running would only confirm the need for worry, for urgency, coming out to the tracks blazing white now with sunlight, where she saw, just above them, smoke rising, then rising higher still.

They hurried up the tracks and then along the road that ran beside the canal, where they were passed by a wailing siren and cars racing after it. Someone finally stopped and said, 'C'mon kids. Get in.' They made it to the mill when it was already cordoned off behind the town's police cars and fire truck and by the crowd who had come to see or help, where burnt shards of wood lay scattered about the far end of the building and the windows were blackened with smoke. Sasha now pushed through, asking, 'Has anyone seen my father? Has anyone seen my father?!' A man led her to the front and said to the fireman standing there, 'Henry, this is Dovonovitch's kid. She's looking for her dad.' The fireman looked at her and might have said something, but she didn't hear it, for she'd already seen the answer in his eyes even before she saw, right after, her father's body being rushed out on a stretcher, his head immobile, no longer held up by pride or rage but kept in place by a white plastic brace, as if to keep it from lolling like a baby's.

*

Everyone knew, or thought they knew, that Jamie Dence was behind the explosion at the mill. It was a general suspicion, unconfirmed, but no less certain because of that. He never acknowledged what they suspected, despite the accusing looks in the weeks that followed, when the mill was shut while they took away the rubble and closed that section of the building where the windows were streaked as black as death. He showed nothing but contempt afterwards for the looks everyone gave him. There were still some who kept his company, a few he would still drink with and laugh at, who might even have admired the flagrant, angry, haughty contempt he showed as time went on and still nothing happened to him: no law invoked, no revenge wreaked. There were two in particular he used to spend his time with that summer: Mike Basha, a thin, needy fellow who was still working at the KFC when most everyone else his age was building something with their lives; and another one who seemed to come out of nowhere that summer, a friend he'd met up north, who'd come and stayed for the summer, then disappeared again not long after the explosion, and who never seemed to speak to anyone but Jamie. They had rented a place together in the cheap duplexes back beyond St Clair's school, where they played music loud late into the night, and got high when they weren't out at the bars. Their neighbours saw them one night – Jamie and his friend from up north – high as kites, dropping a ringing alarm clock from the second-storey window and watching it fall, laughing, then sending poor Basha down to collect it and bring it to them so they could drop it again and again, though no one dared to say anything to them. When one neighbour finally did complain, Jamie appeared at the door, high and sheepish. 'Yeah. Sorry,' he said, jaundiced-looking, the smell of pot reeking inside and the sound of music thumping behind a far, closed door.

But all this partying was before what happened at the mill. He laid much lower after that.

On the day of the accident, he walked into Bud's, alone. He hadn't gone with the others to the mill. He stood at the bar by the other men, appearing to mind his own business before one of the men turned to him and said – not to tell him in particular but announcing the news as he would have to anyone else – 'There was an accident at the mill. The ambulances were up there. The boiler just went off and blew.' Fear flickered vaguely in Jamie's eyes. Because if he'd wanted the explosion, the town debated forever after, he'd probably thought no one would be there.

'When?' he'd asked, calm.

'This afternoon. Didn't you hear about it?'

'I was sleeping,' Jamie said, and everyone looked at him with distaste.

'Dovonovitch was there. He was right close to it when it went off. They rushed him up to Corner Brook. I seen him,' one man almost bragged. 'I could see right inside him…'

'What was Dovonovitch doing up there on Saturday, anyway?' someone else asked.

'Who knows?' They all shrugged. It came out later that he'd gone there, as the foreman, to finish up some extra work over the weekend.

Jamie nodded at the news, a look of fear on his face now, drinking his beer as the men went on debating. Outrage eventually rose up against the managers – the ones no one saw, the ones above Dovonovitch – for having allowed the faulty equipment in the first place. There was righteous indignation, not just for Dovonovitch – for he was briefly forgotten – but for everyone who had to work there, then for those who had been laid off, not just at their mill but across the island, while they, the company owners, continued to cut corners, risk lives and 'make a killing', pun intended!

'They don't give a dam about us, sure they don't,' everyone cried. 'Have you ever looked at the state of the boiler? It was bound to go off!' And it wasn't just the boiler, they agreed, it was every piece of god-forsaken machinery in that place. It was lucky it was only Dovonovitch, when it could have been the whole lot of them, it could have been many, many more.

'Poor Dovonovitch,' someone said.

'Poor Frank…' they agreed.

They continued talking among themselves, filled with outrage and still too concerned with the details of what had only just happened to consider the bigger picture, but when they finally did put things together – the earlier vandalism at the dam, his long absence on the very day of the explosion, the feigned ignorance – Jamie stood at the crosshairs of their swelling outrage with that look, as it were, of pale fear, of startled incredulity, forever frozen on his face.

*

They'd already taken Sasha's father to the hospital by the time Jamie Dence walked into the bar that day. The paramedics had known to take the road directly out of town, away from the small local hospital, and to rush along the highway, the sirens screaming through the trees and startled birds, to the Hospital Emergency Department in Corner Brook. They fed him blood all the while; his whole side had been ripped open and his neck almost snapped by the explosion, in spite of which, as though by force of his pride alone, he still remained conscious. And as they fed him blood and continued to shout above him, a neighbour had followed in his car with Sasha and her mother while another had been assigned to look after the sister who remained, blissfully unaware, in her bedroom back home.

Sasha and her mother sat in the waiting room for several hours. Neither wept.

'He'll be okay, Mom,' she said.

'Yes, dear,' her mother said, stolid, staring at the swinging doors through which her husband's body had passed.

'Can I get you coffee, Mom?'

'No, dear,' she answered, sitting heavily on her seat as if nothing could move her, staring at the door, then turning, as if just now remembering, to smile blandly for her.

A nurse emerged. 'Mrs Dovonovitch?' She glanced at Sasha, who remained quiet beside her mother, and focused her attention back at the older woman: 'I'm afraid it's not good news.'

She was new on the job and explained to them

the situation in jargon that kept the explanation as clinical as could be. Mrs Dovonovitch remained seated, looking at the nurse without understanding exactly what was being said and not asking for more information but understanding, at least, that her husband was still alive.

Sasha got up after and bought a chocolate bar from the candy machine by the entrance and brought it back.

'You should eat, Mom,' she said.

After the nurse had left, Mrs Dovonovitch sat with that same small-town stoicism until, hours later, a doctor came out again and said, 'It's okay. We've gotten through the worst of it,' looking equally at Sasha. 'You can go home. It's best to come back and see him tomorrow,' adding again: 'He's okay.' They went home without seeing him and the next day another neighbour drove Sasha's mother up again while Sasha stayed home to look after her sister. She was happy to help; it distracted her thoughts, gave her something to do. She cooked for and fed her sister, and spoke to her gently when she wondered where Mama was, when she cried for Mama and pushed her food away, throwing it, by accident, to the floor, and crying because of that, until Sasha, holding her, had calmed her again. She cleaned up the food and waited alone in the living room until her mother returned from Corner Brook late.

Her mother continued to go up in the days that followed, and although school had started again,

Sasha remained home to look after her sister. Finally, on the day her father checked out, Sasha went up again. This time when she saw him, his face was cleaned of blood and seemed to sag down beneath the great weight of his skin. His eyes were hard and dark, like stones beneath the water of Bear Lake, and they looked distracted, as though he were absorbed in some place deep within him, heedless of his wife and the orderlies pushing him, and heedless of her. She stood to greet him. He stared at her once with fleeting recognition, then turned his eyes away, his body pushing over the sides of the wheelchair, his cleaned hands, almost as innocent as a child's, limp upon his lap, where they would remain as such until, she understood, she or someone else moved them for him.

IX

Tom watched Sasha recede as he might have watched her on a train slowly parting from his life. When he saw her, he felt like she was someone different, that she was now in some place he could not reach, and that vast, cold winds were snatching the roiled feelings of his heart and dropping them, leaden and useless, in the deadening space between them. It was as though an invisible and irrevocable wall had been set down, separating them from what they had been and what they were now: invisible, because he could still see her; irrevocable, because no matter how much he wanted to yell and scream and beat his fists upon it, he knew that would change nothing.

He would go to see her after dinner in the time he usually studied – walking from his home up to Elizabeth Street in the early autumn dark, his hands in his pockets, his face, lit in the headlights of a passing car, distracted, confused, even angry, not even looking at the car but staring straight ahead. He would walk slowly and certainly up to Sasha's, showing up, unlike before, unannounced, whenever he wanted, rapping on the screen door and waiting a few seconds before he heard the slow scrape of slippers emerging from beyond it. Mrs Dovonovitch would come to greet him. She, alone, had surprised everyone, by neither breaking nor bending under the strain of having now an incapacitated husband, and a house to manage all alone. She would look at Tom with the same large, pale, expressionless blue eyes, no longer surprised to see him there, as she had been the first time he'd come after the accident. 'She's upstairs,' she would tell him, never calling him by his name, not from hostility but as if in allegiance to her now impaired husband, who had never once spoken to him directly. Then she would waddle back into the kitchen, where Tom could hear the TV blaring and where he could see, just inside the frame of the door, the strangely booted feet of her husband lodged on the wheelchair, polished black as stone, and to where Mrs Dovonovitch returned to feed him again.

Once – on his birthday, which Sasha had forgotten, unlike the year before – he found her crying in her room alone. And the expression on her face, when she looked up at him, her eyes red, her tears glistening in the lonely lamplight by her bed, almost ashamed, while the blare of the TV below only seemed to amplify the emptiness of the house – that expression made something (not hurt, but rage, although there was a great deal of hurt in it, too) stab somewhere deep inside of him.

'It was Jamie,' he told her one day, later, having heard the rumours like everyone else.

'Let it go, Tom,' she said.

'I'm not going to let it go, Sash!'

'It's my father, not yours!' she cried angrily, her voice trembling, staring at him until, finally, he looked away.

*

The rumours about Jamie had begun to circle even before Mr Dovonovitch, his flaccid face clenched in silence, his eyes so dark and abstracted they seemed covered with discoloured film, had returned from the hospital. But rather than make Jamie retreat from public scrutiny, the now near-open accusations only appeared to make him rowdier, as though he wanted to show his disdain for such rumours and took enormous pride in doing so. He knew enough to avoid Bud's bar, where many of the workers drank, but he drank at the hotel and at restaurants downtown, without any pretence of trying to hide away from the town's suspicions. He drank with whoever would talk to him, meeting up with Mike Basha, with whom he spent most of his time. He often drank at the pool hall during the days, cutting a foolish figure at his age, and the kids grew more and more wary of him. People began to shun him. But despite his apparent indifference to the rumours circulating about him, there were some times, often when he was hungover after an especially heavy night, that his eyes appeared more darkly circled than before, his face paler, excoriated from growing bitterness: and the violence that had always simmered in him became more apparent.

His friend, Basha, caught the worst of it. A story circulated about Jamie at this time that showed how desperate he had become and proved, whether it had been an accident or not, how much the explosion or the consequent isolation gnawed at him, bringing out something worse in him than had been there before. Some might have even felt some pity for him before this, in the way that, although he was not proven guilty of anything, people now greeted him coldly or didn't greet him at all, so that he began to call out after them, 'How you doing?!' with hard eyes and crowing disdain.

One day, Basha missed his shift at KFC and reported in the next morning with his face ashen, his breath still reeking of booze, his eyes downcast, and ashamed. Mrs Cameron, the manager, had been angrily waiting for him, tapping her toe in rising fury, her fingers splayed on the greasy takeout counter. He came in with his head bowed and barely glanced at her as he hurried to put on his apron. 'I'm sorry, Mrs Cameron. I wasn't feeling too well...' Mrs Cameron, a stout woman who, despite knowing Basha was a layabout, had a soft spot for him, drew in a great breath and was set to harangue him, was even perhaps going to fire him, while he stood waiting for it, meekly accepting it, when she suddenly studied him more closely and saw what she hadn't seen before: the dark welt around his left eye, the crusted blood in his nostril, the black split in his swollen lip.

'Good lord, boy. What happened to you?!'

'It's nothing,' he said angrily, before lowering his tone. 'Jamie and I was just messing around.'

'He did this to you?!'

'We was just messing around... He drank too much...'

They had been at The Balmoral, a dive bar near the outskirts of town, where high-school students mixed with old alcoholics. Jamie had been fine at first, even cheery. They had been sitting with some girls from high school who hadn't heard about him, the jukebox playing loud, and Jamie was more expansive than he had been in a while. He was flirting with one of the young girls, Basha said, when his mood changed after someone came over and whispered in one of the girls' ears, looked at Jamie and left. They heard the drunken girl Jamie was flirting with say, making eyes at him even as her friends dragged her away, 'I don't care what they say about him. I don't care. He's cute...'

Basha watched the girls walk away, and when he looked back he saw, now, how much Jamie's mood had changed. He sat staring darkly before his beer, even as Basha tried to keep up a drunken banter. 'Don't pay no attention to them, Jamie,' he said, hurriedly. 'I bet we could still get one... You sure could get one, no doubt, and maybe even me, if I's lucky... no, Jamie? You think I could get one, one different, maybe?... They sure liked you, huh?... Ha ha ha... What'd you think? Huh, Jamie?... It don't matter, Jamie, it don't matter... We'll get another pitcher, huh, Jamie?' But Jamie continued to sit in stony silence. The more he drank, the darker his face grew, and his mood seemed to push everyone away, as if a clearing was opening up around them. Basha could hear it too, the whispers – 'He did it.' 'Shut up, he'll hear you.' 'He did it.' – as they sat alone and grew drunker and drunker. They drank a great deal while Basha kept babbling on until they got into Basha's old car. He miraculously got them to his apartment on the far side of town, still talking: 'Yeah, this was sure fun, Jamie. I think you shoulda talked to that one, eh?... Still, you don't pay them no mind, what they're saying,' and: 'I know you didn't do it on purpose...' They opened the front door to the apartment and Jamie, who had said nothing for what had seemed like hours, finally said, once they were inside, 'Will you shut the fuck up?'

'I'm sorry, Jamie,' Basha slurred. 'I'm just saying that I don't think—'

Jamie finally broke and struck him once, then, strangely, stopped, then hit him again and again and again and again, until it felt like it wasn't going to end. 'I said shut the fuck up! Shut the fuck up, you fucking idiot! SHUT THE FUCK UP!' he said, striking him until Basha, curled on the floor, was loudly whimpering. Jamie suddenly stopped and looked down at him, angry, but incredulous now too. 'Mmm sorry, Basha…' he mumbled, exhausted, and reached for him but Basha, curled in a ball, pulled his arm away angrily. Jamie stumbled to the couch, among the ashtrays and empty beer cans, and fell immediately asleep.

He left Basha's place early the next day, without Basha asking him to. In fact, Basha told him he didn't have to. 'Hey man, you don't have to go,' he said, sadly. 'It was an accident…' But Jamie only looked at him with hatred, saying nothing, then left. He made no pretence of smiling anymore after that, or of pretending not to care. He drank alone, but no longer boisterously and never too much, standing at the end of the bar without speaking to anyone. He hung out at the pool hall on Main Street during the day, staring at people with violence in his eyes, and making extra money by challenging them, with a threatening glare, to games of pool. He played silently and thoroughly, often beating them. 'Thanks,' he would say, when he took their money, as a strange courtesy; or, on the rare occasions when someone would beat him and decline to take his proffered bills, he would growl, 'Take the money,' until they took it and hurried away in fear. As the weeks passed and everyone decided now to simply ignore him, he grew more isolated, more reticent and more angry, until even his oldest acquaintances had little to do with him anymore. And it was as if then, when he could fall no further in everyone's esteem, including perhaps his own, at a point when people were willing, if not to forgive him, at least to let him be, that something within him, something vicious within him, made him push them, and himself, even further.

*

It was late September. She was walking home alone with bags of groceries for her mother, lost in that world into which she had since withdrawn, when he pulled his car up beside her.

'Hey-hey, Sasha,' he said, leaning across the front seat, and for the first time in a long time, the autumn sunlight reflecting on his oversized sunglasses, Jamie smiled.

X

Tom tried not to think about Jamie at all. Sasha never told him about what was happening – about Jamie's harassment or strange solicitude or whatever you want to call it – because he barely saw her anymore, and when he did, she felt to him like someone different. In the time since the accident, Tom had learned more or less to let her be, telling himself that things would change, that she needed time, fighting back his urge to see her and an almost instinctive belief that he could make it okay. On the empty weeknights – they met now only on the weekends – he would force himself to study but would retain nothing. That earlier ability he'd had to turn away from Sasha in his mind and focus on his books was gone. Instead, he would rise now from his desk, pushing his books away exasperated, and go out into the early autumn night to walk, sometimes pensive, sometimes agitated. Often, without having admitted to himself what he was doing, he would find himself before Sasha's house again, where a light burned behind the front window curtain, and another, like a mooring, shone above her front door.

'I'm sorry. She's at the Bennetts',' – meaning Cindy's – her mother might tell him when he went to knock on her front door, or, 'I'm sorry. She's sleeping,' and he would turn away with the sense of urgency that had driven him there gone and a feeling of enormous emptiness in its place.

One evening he was lucky enough – or unlucky, as he might have told himself – to find her sitting in her living room alone. She answered the door and he knew immediately, upon seeing her, that it had been a mistake to come.

'Hi Tom,' she said, patiently. She stood in the doorway in her pyjamas and a sweatshirt. A schoolbook lay open in a pool of light on the couch behind her.

'I was out for a walk and thought I'd drop by,' he rushed to explain, and as he stepped inside, he felt the night air clinging to his clothes like a guilty conscience. 'I came by before,' he added. He sat beside her on the couch with his jacket still on and talked without stopping and without meaning.

'It's been a while since I've seen you, during the week, I mean, so I figured why not? I hope I'm not bothering you. Am I bothering you? What are you studying? Is that math? You know, I'm pretty good at math, Sash…' he joked, lamely. He took up the book and pretended to look at it in silence and laid it down again on the couch. 'It's been a couple of weeks since I really talked to you,' he repeated, shook his head and laughed again lamely. 'How's school...?'

'It's good...' she said, then apologised: 'I've been really busy.'

'It's okay. You know, I've been busy too. I understand... How's your dad?'

'He's fine...'

'Let me know if there's anything I can do,' he offered, and felt foolish saying it.

She nodded and tried, vainly, to smile.

'Well, I should get going!' He stood up so that he was standing over her now and, without thinking, even as her parents sat close by in the kitchen watching TV, he bent down suddenly and kissed her. She accepted it with dry lips, such as he'd never felt before, then he left.

Yet there were other times when it seemed that her old self was returning, that things between them might become what they had once been.

'I suppose one good thing to come of all this is that it's sure I won't be working at the mill,' he joked with her one Saturday afternoon in October while they were out walking.

'Don't be stupid,' she said and smiled indulgently.

'I'm trying not to be,' he quipped. 'I suppose I could always be the dog-catcher. Ha ha ha.'

She didn't laugh, but she smiled again, which was enough, keeping her hand in his. They walked for a long time in patient silence through the autumn's damp air.

'I've got to go home,' she finally said, withdrawing her hand and putting it back into her jacket pocket. 'It's getting late.'

*

Jamie made no attempt to hide what he was doing but he didn't flaunt it either, for the mere sake of flaunting it, because that, ultimately, was not his purpose. He seemed to be everywhere. He made a point now of smiling at her, even if she was in a crowd of people, at which she would startle and look away. 'Hey Sasha!' he would call out triumphantly, smiling against the angry looks thrown his way from whomever else was around. Ignoring him only seemed to encourage him. After she'd avoided going downtown as much as she possibly could, she found him one day in his car parked on the side of the road she took on her way home from school. She recognised his car from a distance a second time and changed her route, cutting across another road and back up again to Elizabeth Street.

A week or so passed, and he seemed to have disappeared for good. Then several weeks after the overtures had begun, two weeks after she'd avoided going downtown, and one week after she'd changed her route home, he reappeared, leaning against his car on her new route home from school, with his hair newly cut, his long, thin, pale face rising proud from the collar of his fake leather jacket, his ears sticking out from his head, boyishly.

She saw the old blue Mustang shining in the sun as she turned the corner, but she didn't want to give in, she wouldn't turn and flee; determined to continue.

'Hey,' he said as she passed. She walked by without looking at him and without daring to look back, feeling only utter silence trail her.

And still she said nothing to anyone, because she felt it would do no good, because she thought – because she hoped, believed – that it would all eventually stop, as it had before.

The next time she saw Jamie, however – his car parked in the same place, him standing in the same position, waiting for her there, almost as if they'd agreed upon this meeting place, together – he did more than call out.

'Let me take that for you,' he said, pulling her school bag from her shoulder with such abrupt insistence that she let go. It was four in the afternoon and there was no one else on the street. He heaved the bag over his shoulder and she smelt for the first time the overwhelming odour of his cheap cologne.

'Whoah! What's a little girl like you doing carrying a big bag like this?!' He laughed. 'Damn if I ever carried a bag with this much books once in my life! Ha ha!'

'You need a muscle man to help you carry a thing like this,' he said, still trying to joke. 'A real man, ha ha… I got the muscles,' he continued, half-joking, half in earnest. 'See, take a look.' He offered her the arm holding the bag. 'Take a look. Go ahead. C'mon, take a look…' There was a pause, and he stopped. 'You don't look 'cause you believe I did that to your dad,' he said, with a tone of sudden, startling intimacy. 'You believe what everyone else says, don't you?… Do you think I would do something like that? Do you think I would do something like that on purpose? Huh?! Do you?! Do I look like that kind of guy to you?' He stood on the street, one clenched arm holding up her bag, and his voice was quieter, distant and angry.

'No,' she said, having stopped, her voice in her throat. She forced herself to look at him, so as not to let herself be cowed, to appear stronger than she felt.

'Good. 'Cause I'm not. I didn't think you'd think that,' he said. They'd reached the corner of her street at the top of the hill and he handed her back her bag. 'I'm glad we understand each other,' he said. It looked for a moment like he might try to kiss her, but ultimately, he didn't. 'I'll see you around, okay, Sasha?'

She almost crumbled when he left, but she managed to wait until she got home and closed her bedroom door before she wept for a long time, over many things, alone.

But still she kept things to herself; still she said nothing to Tom about it, on the weekends when they met, in what had even become, for both of them, the obligation of seeing each other. For she couldn't see it getting any worse. He would, she thought, just go away.

*

There was something wrong, Tom knew, but he couldn't say what. Sasha appeared even more worn down. The colour had left her face, she seemed to put up with his visits patiently and seemed, at the same time, by a sort of frail silence, to want him to stay. They never walked far from her place. She didn't want to go downtown anymore. She never came to his. And then one weekend Tom spied Jamie loitering on Main Street, standing apparently carefree in the sunlight, and he suddenly remembered the moment he'd walked into Sasha's room and found her crying alone, and remembered the distance growing between them, and remembered how things had been before and the pain of how they were now: and rage rose within him. Jamie stood on the sidewalk before Home Hardware, smoking placidly, his face raised to the sun, as though he were unaffected by the opprobrium the town had laid upon him, as though he were thumbing his nose at the whole silent weight of their judgement – and the idea of it became, for Tom, unbearable. Each time he thought of Jamie afterwards, his rage deepened. One day not long after – one Saturday when he was still trying vainly to reach out to Sasha – he was unable to bear it anymore and blurted out as they were walking in silence through the same, empty streets near her house, with the feeling of something ending, or, rather, he knew, having already ended:

'I saw Jamie Dence the other day...'

*

It was the third week of October. Jamie was still paying her attention, but the tone had changed: he was less aggressive now; more solicitous. He had shown up in front of her school with a bouquet: cheap, withered flowers he had splurged on with his meagre welfare, wrapped, by the town's sole florist, in purple paper and a white ribbon, upon the ordering of which the florist had looked at Jamie with surprise, then handed them to him coldly, his face pale, outraged at the idea of this man buying flowers for anyone, this man who he and the whole town just wished would go away.

'These are for your dad,' Jamie told her, reaching into his front seat and thrusting them at her while looking away, as though he were forcing himself to do this. He got into his car without another word and drove off, and she felt, despite herself, almost pity for him. But a few days later, while she was downtown in the grocery mart shopping for her mom, he suddenly appeared beside her again, the cheap stink of his cologne rising in her nostrils before she saw him.

'Those nuts over there are cheaper,' he said from behind, startling her. 'I buy those ones there. They're just as good. You just ain't paying for some fancy name. It's all the same!' he sneered, angry.

A man from the town saw them standing there, saw the pallor on Sasha's face, and came over to them.

'Are you okay?' he asked Sasha, looking darkly at Jamie, but Jamie stood where he was, staring back, holding his ground.

'Hi, Mr Brown,' Sasha said quietly.

'Are you okay?' Mr Brown, the gym teacher at her high school, repeated, looking at Jamie again.

'I'm okay,' she said, 'but could you give me a ride home?'

In his truck afterwards, with her bag of groceries on her lap, he asked, 'Is that fellow giving you trouble?'

'It's nothing,' she said, and added nothing more.

'It's best to stay away from the likes of him,' he told her. They'd arrived at her house. 'You let me know if he's causing you any trouble. One of these days, he's going to get what's coming to him.'

It was on the evening of that same Saturday that Tom, eyeing her carefully, said, 'I saw Jamie Dence the other day...' When Sasha ignored it, he continued peevishly. 'He was walking downtown, smoking a cigarette, without a worry in the world.' Her stubborn silence bothered him, and he began to grow angrier. 'No one was saying anything to him, not that he cares. Not a worry in the world.' He looked at her fiercely. 'Doesn't that bother you?!'

She met his sudden fierceness with the same star-tled expression she might have used, once, with Jamie.

'Everyone knows he did it, Sasha... The whole town hates him but no one's doing anything about it. It was him who blew up the boiler at the mill. It was him who screwed around with the dam last year. He did the same thing at the mill, but this time it worked. I've talked to people – they know. I don't care if they can't prove it, it was him! He did it! He did it! He did it!' Tom insisted, growing angrier and angrier. 'He can't get away with it!'

She stared at him, troubled by the violence in his eyes, in his voice.

'Leave it alone...' she pleaded with him quietly.

'It's not fair!' Tom shouted like a child, sounding suddenly much younger than he was. 'Look at him! No – look at me! Look at you! Look at your father, Sasha! Look what he did to your father!' he cried, carried away now, going too far. 'Look at us!'

It was all too much for her – the obvious end between them, Jamie, her father's daily, heavy, silent rage – and, finally, she broke.

'Let it be, Tom. Please, please, please, let it be,' she begged. Hot tears were streaming down her face and she was trembling with all the grief she finally allowed now to rise up in her. 'I don't want any more hurt,' she sobbed. 'Please let it go, Tom, please!'

But he didn't.

*

The beginning of the end came like this: Tom showed up one evening at Cindy's doorstep. 'There's a boy at the door for you,' her mother came up to her room and told her, and when she went down, she found Tom, pale, hollowed out, beneath the porch light where the last stray moths of the season thumped weakly.

'Did you know Jamie's been harassing Sasha?' he demanded.

'No,' she said wearily, then: 'What are you going to do, Tom – beat him up? Ha ha.' She laughed, but his look made her uneasy.

'Well, he is,' Tom said coldly. He looked wasted, as if he hadn't eaten in days, and his eyes twitched beneath the shadowed light while he stared fiercely, as if waiting for her to do or say something more.

She grew worried.

'What are you going to do, Tom?... Tom?' she called out after him, for he had already turned with that same expression and walked away.

*

Sasha found out about what was going to happen through Cindy. Weeks had gone by since she had heard from Tom. She wondered in her silence if she had been too hard on him, and the rare times that the phone rang, her heart thrilled at the expectation that her mother might say, 'Sasha, it's for you,' but she never did. Perhaps she should have told him. Perhaps he would have listened. He had a good heart, she knew. It was her own weakness, she worried, her own fear and desire to put this all behind her, to not make it worse, that in the end had only shut him out, too. In the meantime, she went to school and did her homework and tended to her father, who sat in his wheelchair like a great weight in the middle of the house, the body seeming to melt into more of a thick inert mass almost daily – unspeaking, as if his tongue had been broken with his spine, his brown hair neatly, ridiculously combed by her mother, over eyes that burned with rage. She was saved the embarrassment of washing him by a nurse who came three times a week, paid for by the state and donations from neighbours, but she sometimes had to help him to the toilet. He had said almost nothing since the accident, but only stared ahead with darkened eyes and a dark, thickening face. She was feeding him as her mother tended to her sister in the other room when she heard someone rap at the front door and her heart thrilled at the thought that finally, now, after two weeks of silence, Tom was back. She heard her mother shuffle towards the front door, then come back up the hallway, not towards her sister's room but towards the kitchen, towards her.

'Cindy's here,' her mother said, and Sasha felt her heart drop.

Tom had spoken about Jamie to a few friends at school and, several days after he had appeared on

Cindy's doorstep, Cindy had made enquiries to find out the heart of the matter and had come now to tell Sasha about it.

'Tom's going after Jamie Dence,' she said.

'What?' Sasha said, having come from the kitchen to the front hall, wiping her hands. Her face paled with fear.

The house was filled with the oppressive silence of her incapacitated father and the small barking of the TV from the kitchen. The front room, to the left of where they stood, lay empty, with a sole lamp lighting the gloom in the corner.

'He found out Jamie's been talking to you. Why didn't you tell me, Sasha?'

'That was ending,' Sasha said. 'That was going to end! I told him to leave it be!'

That was Thursday evening in the very beginning of November. The autumn night covered the town like a black kettle and you could already smell winter high in the air.

'Where is he?' Sasha asked.

'I don't know.' Cindy shrugged, for any danger, as she saw it, was now being averted. 'Probably at home. He'll be okay, Sash.'

Sasha looked back into the kitchen, then went to the back of the house to get her jacket. 'Mom, I've got to go out for a moment,' she said at her sister's door.

'Okay Sasha,' her mother said mechanically.

'I'll be back in an hour.'

'Okay Sasha.'

'I won't be too long. I promise, Mom,' Sasha told her.

'Mm.'

She put on her jacket and walked with Cindy to the end of the street, then hurriedly but heavily continued alone down the hill, like someone constrained, trying not to run – towards Tom's, towards the Clairebournes'.

Tom looked surprised when he found her at the back door. 'What are you doing here?'

'Can I come in?'

They went to his room and once the door was closed, she blurted out, 'I heard you were going to go after Jamie!'

She left a half-hour later, calmed by his reassurances. It was only the next evening, when she remembered what she had not paid attention to the night before – namely, that he had let her walk home alone – and recalled his peevish 'Who told you that?' and the false note in his 'Sash, I wouldn't do that,' that she suddenly admitted to herself that he was lying.

She waited as long as she could stand the next morning, attending first to her chores, before she went to his house.

'Is Tom here?'

Mrs Clairebourne looked at her curiously and without warmth.

'No.'

'C-can I come in? I forgot something in his room,' Sasha said, blushing at her lie. But she noticed nothing out of place in his room beyond the pile of envelopes on his desk that she had noticed in passing the night before. She rode all over town to look for him and came to Cindy's afterwards, shaken. 'I can't find him! I don't know where he is!' And it was after she left Cindy, when she remembered the empty envelopes, that she remembered the clearing they used to go to by the chute and then remembered too the dam nearby and sped off past the school, down the dirt road, on and on, leaving the chute to the side, then speeding further again. She saw the Mustang parked on the road beside the dam, shining in the sunlight, before she saw them.

She saw them struggling by the valve house and cried, 'Tom!' but they didn't hear her. 'Tom!' she cried again, throwing down her bike and jumping over the gate to where they were wrestling, crying, 'Stop it! Stop it!' running towards where Jamie still had in his back pocket the unsigned letter that read, 'I know what you did. I can prove it,' and the meeting date and place. Tom, who had already since lost his nerve but who was stronger than Jamie had supposed, was wrestling with him, so that the two were pushing and pulling each other almost equally, just inside the dam, against the barred ledge. She arrived behind them and cried out again 'Tom!' and Jamie turned and Tom pushed and she alone was the one who managed to take hold of Jamie before he fell over the ledge. The two struggled to hold on, for Tom too had fallen over but was clinging to the bar; and when Jamie, still dangling, looked up at her, where she lay dragged upon the concrete so that her breast was bleeding and where the wind seemed to roar about her head and the distance down was dizzying, then smiled, she felt, like a shudder, the image of her father and his dark eyes rise up before her, she felt all the pain and all the fear, then opened her hand and let go.

PART FOUR

XI

They came to Cindy's house afterwards because they couldn't go home – not to Tom's, not to Sasha's, and so they came to Cindy's. Sasha sat unspeaking on Cindy's bed, her eyes staring ahead in horror as though at some indelible spot in the air.

'There was an accident at the dam. Jamie fell. He was holding on to Sasha and he fell,' Tom explained, his face pale and deadly serious but his eyes still grappling with the enormity of what had happened. He left her with Cindy and returned to the dam and came back several hours later. It was only luck that it rained the next day, washing away anything suspicious. It continued to rain for a long time, so that days passed before anyone found Jamie, lying below where his neck had snapped, and from where he looked up, his mouth agape, as though still startled at the passing sky.

That there was little sympathy for Jamie, either before or after, played no small part in what followed. The town greeted his sudden and mysterious disappearance with indifference. Many believed in the beginning that he'd started drinking too much again and gone off on a bender. A few days had passed when his one and only friend, Mike Basha, ventured to the apartment Jamie had been renting monthly on the outskirts of town and peered through the window, but seeing the empty beer cans on the table, and the overflowing ashtrays, and with no lights on, he, like everyone else, had also thought that Jamie had gone off drinking again, probably to Corner Brook, maybe up north. About a week later the body was finally discovered. The understanding of what happened was simple and Jamie was buried without much ceremony: he had fallen, he had likely been drunk, everyone agreed, and that was that.

*

Sasha spent the next year in Bear Lake alone, after Tom graduated and went to St John's to begin studying for medical school. He was finally going to leave! They had spoken about what happened only once. It was Tom who inadvertently broached the subject and seemed most relieved when it was over. He hadn't yet gone off to university, but Sasha was probably already feeling the distance he was putting between them. It was late summer, he'd long been accepted into university in St John's and they were out walking. He was glancing at her shamefully as they walked, his face slightly reddened, because he already felt that he was in this now by obligation alone, that a whole new future was opening up before him and that he was going off to start a new life that Sasha could not and would not be a part of. The dusk glowed purple over the evergreens.

'It's a beautiful evening,' he said, looking for something to say as they walked along Main Street.

'Yeah. I love summer nights,' she said quietly, happy. 'How's school?'

'It's good. I'm getting ready. I've got to drive up with my mom next week to look at where I'm staying.'

They walked in silence. People passed and said, 'Hello.' The town was peaceful.

He felt a wave of desire washing over him, mercifully obliterating his doubts about their future, and he took her hand in his.

'Let's go picnic by the chute tomorrow. It's been a long time since we've been up...' he heard himself saying, then remembered where it was towards and stopped. Sasha's brow knotted. He blanched at his mistake and looked at her, helpless. 'Sorry...' he said. But she conceded, for him. 'Okay,' she said, hugging his arm, and they walked on down Main Street, like lovers.

He hardly came back the first year after he left and always found excuses for not ringing her as often as she would have liked. When he came back for Christmas holidays, a full day passed before he called her, although she was excitedly waiting for his call. He gave the excuse that he had to spend time with his mother.

'You never call, Tom…' she reproached him on the phone, half-teasing, and was surprised by his embarrassed reply.

'I'm busy,' he mumbled. 'I've got a lot of work.'

It was during his second summer home that he finished it, having come back for a two-week stay before returning to St John's to work. He'd changed much in the two years since he'd left, having adopted the laissez-faire demeanour of the other St John's students, with a thin beard on his face, and his hair grown out and messy. He seemed distant, and less mature.

'Sash, I can't do this anymore,' he told her, trying to make her understand, his eyes cast down in shame.

'Okay…'

'I-I'm hardly going to be coming back to Bear Lake. I mean, I'm working in St John's for the summer and then I'll be there all year and I don't know when I'll be back. It's not fair on you.'

She nodded. Tears welled up in her eyes but she wouldn't cry in front of him, she wouldn't.

'You've got your dad here, Sash, and I don't know if I'm ever going to be coming back. You've got to look after him, right? I mean, I'll be back to visit, I'll see you when I'm visiting…'

The tears came anyway, rolling down her cheeks as she stood listening to him, and she even, with a weak, trembling smile, let him wipe them away.

'Okay…'

She was eighteen then. She settled in Bear Lake, eventually going to Corner Brook for nursing school but returning to Bear Lake two years later to stay, remaining even after the mill closed down for good and the town passed, through the years, from abandon and dilapidation to something smaller, neater, but more modern, more efficient and, in its own way, for those who grew up there now, lively – still hemmed in by the pine trees and the lake, around which she would often be seen jogging early in the morning, up like a sole lark, alone.

She jogged for years, every morning, further and further, around the edges of the Bear Lake. She wanted to leave but she thought she had to stay for her family – for her mother, her father and her sister. Eventually, she joined the church and started running less – not, that is, the one where most everyone else went but the Catholic one, as though she were still following Tom, as though that was in a way a final turning of her back on her family, after she'd returned and dutifully, without complaining, and still alone, looked after them, even after she'd bought her own house on the other side of town, where she moved between looking after them and driving up to Corner Brook several times a week for nursing.

People began to say bad things about her, but it made her happy. Or at least it put the hope of peace back in her eyes, trembling like a leaf on a branch still clinging against the winds she never talked about battering within her. She even went when Tom was there and would meet her with embarrassment. She continued to go even when, after many years had passed and he was a surgeon on the mainland, he'd returned for a visit with his new wife. 'Hi Sash...' he said, with the same look of embarrassment and even a little pity, but she remained, with her heart breaking. She did not scream, 'You are a hypocrite and a liar and you left me when—' but instead only said, 'Hi,' and shook his hand gently, then shook his wife's hand, then reached out and gently touched the hand of their three-month-old child. 'Poor Sasha,' Tom's mother said after, in a tone of voice that prevented anyone saying anything more about it: but even after that, she kept going, more and more, retreating into the Church so much, with her sad, frail air, that in her last years, few people saw her at all.

*

Everyone treated her with sympathy at first, then pity, then reproach – for the town knew, everyone always knew, what had really happened at the dam years before. It was never said outright, but it came out little by little, as when, for example, her parents were at the other church, with her father still glowering in his wheelchair, while Sasha was up in Tom's old one, where even there people saw her fervency – her rosary, the weekly then daily masses, her singular relationship with the old priest – as being in bad taste: 'She wasn't quite so pious when Jamie Dence was still alive…' There was no proof, but there was small-town certainty, which is stronger than proof. At her funeral, when, at twenty-eight, it was all finally over, from a car crash on her way back from Corner Brook one winter, people admitted as much. Mrs Ball summed it up best when she stood over her casket and shook her head. 'The good Lord has pity on us all,' she said.

*

Cormic returned many years later, driving after a business trip in St John's down to Corner Brook, then down through the valley to Bear Lake. He found his old house on Elizabeth Street just as it had been, and the Brichards still there, but Tom had long gone, as had Sasha, and the only person left that he really knew was Cindy. She lived in a neat, modern complex built on the east side of town, where the beach used to be, bordering the far shore of the lake, and there she filled him in on what had happened after he'd left. She told him it straight, and didn't leave anything out.

She worked now in an old shop on Main Street, among the whitewashed store fronts, and had never married. Her hair was dyed a tinny blond, the colour of burnished silver, but her face was much the same: stern, intolerant, confident, still pretty. She still smoked, and dropped her ashes into an ashtray on a stand by the sofa-chair in which she now sat with a kind of isolate fury. Life's disappointments had lined her face, but she sat non-resigned, still combative; at times, even tender.

'I used to see her a lot, after Tom left, in those first years,' she told him, 'but eventually we drifted apart.' They had sat for the better part of the afternoon and dusk was now falling outside, spreading light out over the water and sky. There swelled an immense silence.

'It'd been years since we'd really talked,' she told him now, about the very end, 'and I literally ran into her outside the new Dominion supermarket, by the highway. "Sash!" I cried, and we briefly spoke before I had to run off, 'cause I had things to do – this was about a week before her accident – something stupid, like getting my hair cut, ha ha! "I'll see you next weekend," I told her, and was planning to, because I never thought I'd never see her again.

'"Okay," she said, standing outside the supermarket with her hands full of groceries, and I remember that for the first time in a long time, much in the way she used to do when she was young, she'd looked at me then and smiled.'

Acknowledgements

Thank you to Louise Boland and Urška Vidoni, for their extraordinary editing skills.

Bookclub and writers' circle notes for the
Fairlight Moderns can be found at
www.fairlightmoderns.com

Share your thoughts about the
book with **#AtlanticWinds**

Also in the Fairlight Moderns series

More coming soon...

SOPHIE VAN LLEWYN

Bottled Goods

*Longlisted for **People's Book Prize for Fiction 2018** and
The Republic of Consciousness Prize 2019*

When Alina's brother-in-law defects to the West,
she and her husband become persons of interest to
the secret services and both of their careers come
grinding to a halt.

As the strain takes its toll on their marriage,
Alina turns to her aunt for help – the wife of a
communist leader and a secret practitioner of the
old folk ways.

Set in 1970s communist Romania, this novella-
in-flash draws upon magic realism to weave a
captivating tale of everyday troubles.

*'It is a story to savour, to smile at, to
rage against and to weep over.'*
—Zoe Gilbert, author of *FOLK*

*'Sophie van Llewyn has brought light
into an era which cast a long shadow.'*
—Joanna Campbell, author of
Tying Down the Lion

Minutes f

Hakim, a Pakista
the streets. Patri
with aspirations c
Moroccan beauti
Saeed, a respected E

Taking place across
Minutes from the Mir
retelling of the virt

'Sabbagh gives
expect: a small pla

di
—Adnan Mah

Hou

'Sabbagh is the R K
—Christop

NIAL GIACOMELLI

The Therapist

*'I am levitating above the curvature of the earth.
Weightless, unencumbered. Flung like a comet out of
the atmosphere and into some great beyond.'*

In this bittersweet and hauntingly surreal tale, a
couple finds the distance between them mirrored
in a strange epidemic sweeping the globe. Little by
little, each victim becomes transparent, their heart
beating behind a visible rib cage, an intricate
network of nerves left hanging in mid-air. Finally,
the victims disappear entirely, never to be
seen again.

'I dreamt that we were at sea,' she says.

Praise for the *Fairlight Moderns:*

*'A delectable compilation of modern
novellas from writers all over the globe.'*
—The Big Issue

OMAR SABBAGH

Minutes from the Miracle City

Hakim, a Pakistani taxi driver whizzing through the streets. Patrick, a Ugandan security guard with aspirations of becoming a writer. Farida, a Moroccan beautician hoping for a fresh start. Saeed, a respected Emirati journalist just back from London.

Taking place across the last few days of Ramadan, *Minutes from the Miracle City* is a fresh and unique retelling of the virtuoso project that is Dubai.

'Sabbagh gives us something we do not expect: a small place packed with complex dwellers.'
—Adnan Mahmutović, author of
How to Fare Well and Stay Fair

'Sabbagh is the RK Narayan of our times.'
—Christopher Jackson,
poet and biographer